Berlin's Underground Network

Hatty Jones

Published by Mick Jobe, 2024.

This is a work of fiction. Similarities to real people, places, or events are entirely coincidental.

BERLIN'S UNDERGROUND NETWORK

First edition. November 11, 2024.

Copyright © 2024 Hatty Jones.

ISBN: 979-8227657244

Written by Hatty Jones.

Berlin's Underground Network
An old Cold War bunker becomes the center of a modern mystery.

Berlin, a city steeped in history, is known for its vibrant streets, iconic landmarks, and layers of stories hidden beneath its surface. But for the Edmondson siblings—Emma, Max, Leo, Sophie, and Ava—Berlin's most captivating tales lie far below ground, in the shadowy depths of its underground network.

It all began with a curious invitation: an exclusive tour of Berlin's historic tunnels, promising a glimpse into the city's Cold War past. For the Edmondsons, seasoned adventurers with a knack for uncovering secrets, it sounded like the perfect family outing. But what started as a routine exploration quickly unravelled into something far more dangerous—and extraordinary.

An unusual door concealed behind graffiti. A cryptic map fragment. A Cold War-era journal filled with symbols no one could decipher. Each discovery pulled the siblings deeper into a mystery that would challenge their wits, their courage, and their trust in one another.

As they navigate Berlin's twisting tunnels, they uncover a trail of hidden bunkers, secret codes, and long-lost technology—clues that point to an enigmatic relic known as the "Berlin Key." But they're not the only ones searching. A ruthless group of treasure hunters, driven by greed, will stop at nothing to claim the prize, and the Edmondsons soon find themselves in a race against time to protect a secret that could change the world.

Beneath the streets of Berlin lies a web of forgotten stories and untold power, guarded by traps, puzzles, and the shadows of history. To uncover the truth, the Edmondsons must rely on their bond as siblings, their courage in the face of danger, and their belief that some secrets are worth protecting.

"Berlin's Underground Network" is a gripping adventure filled with twists, danger, and the timeless question: how far would you go to protect what matters most?

Chapter 1: The Invitation

The sky over Berlin was a pale grey, the kind of overcast that seemed to settle over the city like a blanket, softening its sharp angles and historic facades. The Edmondson siblings stood at the edge of Alexanderplatz, their excitement tempered by the brisk chill in the air. Emma, the eldest and self-designated leader, clutched a letter in her hand, its edges worn from the many times they'd read it on their journey.

"Are you sure this isn't some kind of prank?" Max asked, peering over her shoulder as they reread the invitation for the hundredth time.

"It doesn't look like a prank," Emma said firmly, though her furrowed brow betrayed her uncertainty. "It's too detailed. Who would go to this much trouble just for a joke?"

The letter had arrived at their home two weeks ago, sealed in an unmarked envelope. The typewritten message inside had been brief and enigmatic, inviting the family to participate in an "exclusive tour" of Berlin's underground tunnels, with promises of historical insights and access to places few had ever seen. There was no sender's name, only a time and meeting place listed at the bottom.

"Exclusive, my foot," Sophie muttered, hugging her coat tightly around her. "This could be anyone trying to lure us into some weird tourist trap."

Leo, always the tech-savvy one, tapped away on his phone, scrolling through search results for the name of the company mentioned in the letter. "There's nothing online about 'Berlin's Hidden Passage Tours,'" he said, frowning. "No reviews, no website. It's like this company doesn't exist."

"Which makes it more intriguing," Ava chimed in, her notebook already open, her pencil poised to sketch. "Think about it—what if they're showing us something secret, something that's not in any guidebook?"

Max snorted. "Or what if they're showing us the inside of a scam?"

"We're here, aren't we?" Emma said, cutting through the bickering. "Let's at least see who shows up. If it feels sketchy, we leave. No harm, no foul."

The others nodded reluctantly. The invitation had been compelling enough to convince their parents, who were back at the hotel, to let the siblings explore on their own. Their family had a knack for stumbling into adventure—or, as their parents called it, "trouble."

Emma checked her watch. They were early. The designated meeting point, an old kiosk near the entrance to an S-Bahn station, was bustling with commuters and tourists. The siblings stood in a loose circle, their eyes scanning the crowd for anyone who might look out of place.

"What kind of person sends a mysterious invitation and doesn't even describe themselves?" Sophie asked, her breath fogging in the cold air.

"Someone who wants to stay anonymous," Leo said, still glued to his phone. "Or someone who likes drama."

Before anyone could respond, a man approached them. He was tall and wiry, dressed in a plain grey coat that blended almost perfectly with the backdrop of the city. His hair was salt-and-pepper, his eyes sharp and restless, darting between each sibling as though cataloguing their faces.

"You're early," he said, his voice clipped and businesslike. "Good."

Emma stepped forward, holding up the letter. "Did you send this?"

The man didn't answer immediately. Instead, he reached into his coat and pulled out a laminated badge, which he held up for them to see. The name "Erich Volker" was printed beneath a logo featuring interlocking gears—an emblem that matched the letter's letterhead.

"I represent a group dedicated to preserving Berlin's hidden history," he said, his accent crisp and precise. "The invitation was sent on our behalf."

"And what exactly is this tour about?" Max asked, folding his arms.

Erich's lips twitched into a faint smile, though it didn't reach his eyes. "It's about access. The tunnels beneath Berlin are vast and complex, filled with remnants of the city's past—some well-known, others... less so. My group has spent years mapping and documenting them, and we occasionally invite select individuals to see parts of the network that are normally off-limits."

"Why us?" Sophie asked, suspicion clear in her voice.

Erich hesitated for the briefest of moments, his eyes flicking to Emma before settling on the group as a whole. "Your family has a reputation," he said finally. "You have a knack for uncovering the unusual, for solving puzzles. We thought you'd appreciate the challenge."

Emma felt a flicker of both pride and caution. Their past adventures had earned them plenty of strange looks and even stranger opportunities, but this felt different—bigger, somehow.

"And what's the catch?" Leo asked.

Erich's smile returned, thinner this time. "No catch. Just curiosity and the willingness to explore. If you're interested, meet me tomorrow at 10 a.m. at this address." He handed Emma a small card with an address scribbled on it in neat handwriting. "We'll begin the tour there."

"And if we're not interested?" Max asked, narrowing his eyes.

"Then you're free to walk away," Erich said simply. "But something tells me you won't."

With that, he turned on his heel and disappeared into the crowd, leaving the siblings standing in stunned silence.

"Well, that wasn't suspicious at all," Sophie said after a long pause.

"I think it was intriguing," Ava countered, already sketching Erich's sharp features in her notebook. "He didn't give too much away, which makes me want to know more."

Emma studied the card in her hand, her mind racing. The address was in Mitte, not far from their current location. It looked ordinary enough, but she couldn't shake the feeling that there was more to this than Erich was letting on.

"What do you think, Em?" Max asked, watching her carefully.

"I think..." Emma began, then trailed off, glancing at each of her siblings in turn. "I think we should check it out. But carefully."

"Carefully," Sophie echoed. "Famous last words."

Leo shrugged. "It's not like we have anything better to do."

The group fell into step, heading back toward the hotel to prepare for whatever lay ahead. None of them said it aloud, but the air between them buzzed with anticipation. The invitation, the tunnels, the mysterious Erich—it all felt like the beginning of something bigger.

As they walked, Ava flipped to a fresh page in her notebook, jotting down the words that had been rattling in her head since Erich's arrival: Curiosity and the willingness to explore. It sounded like an invitation to adventure—or a warning.

Only time would tell which one it was.

Chapter 2: A Hidden Door

The underground air was damp and cool, carrying a faint metallic tang that seemed to cling to the walls. The Edmondsons followed closely behind the guide as he led them through the tunnels, his flashlight casting long, flickering shadows. The concrete walls were layered with history: faded stencils of Cold War propaganda, colorful graffiti tags from recent decades, and even older, crumbling bricks from the days of Berlin's original underground railway.

Emma walked at the front of the group, her eyes scanning the surroundings for anything unusual. Behind her, Max trailed, his hands in his pockets, a sceptical look etched on his face. Sophie, Leo, and Ava brought up the rear, whispering to each other about the stories the guide had shared earlier—tales of escape routes, forgotten bunkers, and tunnels that stretched far beyond what the city's official maps acknowledged.

"This section was once part of an emergency system during the Cold War," the guide said, his voice echoing faintly in the narrow passage. "A network of tunnels designed to shelter people in the event of an attack. It was abandoned after reunification, but much of it remains intact."

Leo raised his hand. "How much of this is mapped?"

The guide hesitated for a moment before answering. "Most of it, officially. But there are areas that have been sealed off or forgotten over time. The city's underground is larger and more complex than people realize."

"Forgotten?" Ava asked, scribbling in her notebook. "Or hidden?"

The guide smiled faintly but didn't respond.

As they continued walking, Max lagged slightly behind, his gaze fixed on the walls. Something about the layers of graffiti caught his attention. Amidst the colorful tags and chaotic scrawls, a faint outline of a rectangular shape seemed to emerge—a door, almost entirely concealed by paint and grime.

"Hey, wait a second," Max called, stopping abruptly.

The group turned to look at him as he stepped closer to the wall, tilting his head to examine the markings. "This isn't just a random patch of graffiti. Look at the edges—it's too clean. This is a door."

Emma moved beside him, squinting at the wall. The shape he pointed to was subtle but unmistakable: the faint outline of a metal frame embedded in the concrete. The graffiti layered over it made it easy to miss, but up close, the straight lines gave it away.

"Good catch," Emma said, running her hand along the edge. The texture was different from the surrounding wall—smooth and metallic beneath the chipped paint. "It's sealed, though. No handle or anything."

The guide approached, his expression shifting slightly. "That's nothing," he said quickly. "Just a maintenance panel. Probably hasn't been opened in decades."

"It doesn't look like a maintenance panel," Max said, raising an eyebrow. "It's way too big. And why would you need to graffiti over a maintenance panel?"

The guide stiffened, then shrugged. "People paint whatever they want down here. It's not important."

"But it could be," Ava said, stepping forward. "What's behind it?"

"Nothing of interest," the guide replied curtly. "Please, stay with the group. We need to keep moving."

His tone had changed—sharp and almost defensive. Emma exchanged a glance with Max, who was now more curious than ever. "If it's nothing," Max said, "then why is it sealed? And why cover it up?"

The guide didn't answer. Instead, he turned on his heel and continued walking, gesturing for the group to follow. "This way, please. We're on a tight schedule."

The siblings lingered for a moment, studying the door. Leo crouched down, his flashlight aimed at the base. "Look at this," he whispered. "There's no rust on the edges. It hasn't been here as long as the rest of this tunnel."

Emma nodded, her mind racing. "It's been sealed recently."

"Do you think it's part of the Cold War stuff?" Sophie asked. "Like a hidden bunker or something?"

"Or something newer," Max said, standing and brushing his hands off. "Whatever it is, he doesn't want us asking about it."

"Exactly," Emma said, her voice low. "And that makes it even more interesting."

The sound of footsteps echoed back toward them. The guide had stopped and was looking at them impatiently. "Please stay with the group," he called. "The tunnels can be disorienting if you stray."

"Coming!" Emma said quickly, motioning for the others to follow. As they walked, she whispered to Max, "Remember where this is. We're not done with it."

Max gave a slight nod, a determined glint in his eye. "Like I could forget."

The guide led them deeper into the tunnel system, resuming his carefully rehearsed stories about Berlin's underground history. But the siblings were only half-listening now. Their thoughts kept returning to the hidden door, its edges clean and its surface deliberately obscured. It wasn't just a forgotten relic of the past. It was something far more deliberate—and far more recent.

As they moved further into the tunnels, the guide's voice faded into the background, replaced by the quiet hum of their own curiosity. They didn't know what lay behind that door, but one thing was certain: they would be coming back to find out.

Chapter 3: The Whispering Tunnel

The narrow tunnels seemed to stretch endlessly, their walls slick with condensation and layered with decades of grime. The Edmondsons followed the guide deeper into the underground network, but their earlier focus on his commentary had waned. Their discovery of the hidden door lingered in their minds, a tantalizing question that refused to be ignored.

Leo trailed a few steps behind the group, his recording equipment in hand. He had been quietly capturing the sounds of the tunnels, fascinated by the echoes and the distant, almost imperceptible noises that seemed to pulse through the air. It was a habit he had picked up during their adventures—listening for the hidden, the overlooked.

Ahead, the guide stopped in front of a rusted gate, secured with a thick padlock. He turned to the group, launching into another explanation about Cold War-era safety measures, but Leo wasn't listening. Instead, he adjusted the sensitivity of his microphone, his brows furrowing as he noticed a faint blip on the device's screen.

The sound wasn't part of the usual background noise. It was rhythmic—sharp bursts of static, then silence, then more bursts. Leo tilted his head, moving the microphone toward one of the side passages branching off from the main tunnel. The screen flickered again, the signal growing stronger.

"What are you doing?" Sophie whispered, noticing that Leo had stopped walking.

"Shh," Leo murmured, holding up a hand. "There's something here."

Sophie frowned, glancing toward the others, who were now clustered around the guide. She moved closer to Leo, following his gaze down the darkened passageway. It was one of many offshoots the group had passed, each one marked as off-limits by faded warning signs or piles of rubble.

"What do you mean, 'something'?" she asked quietly.

Leo tapped the screen of his recorder, showing her the faint blips. "There's a signal—or a frequency. It's not random. Look."

Sophie leaned in, squinting at the screen. "Could it be interference? Something from aboveground?"

Leo shook his head. "Not this far down. And it's not coming from where we're walking. It's coming from down there." He pointed toward the side passage, his flashlight illuminating a long, dark corridor that seemed to stretch endlessly into the shadows.

"You're not thinking of going in there, are you?" Sophie asked, her voice dropping into a warning tone.

"Not yet," Leo said, though the curiosity in his voice was unmistakable. "I just want to get closer."

Before Sophie could protest, Leo took a cautious step toward the passage. He adjusted his headphones, the faint bursts of sound growing clearer as he moved. Sophie hesitated, then followed, muttering under her breath about bad ideas.

The side passage was narrower than the main tunnel, the air cooler and heavier. The walls were lined with metal supports, rusted and worn, but still intact. The rhythmic bursts of static in Leo's headphones became sharper, accompanied by a faint hum that he could almost feel rather than hear.

"This place is supposed to be abandoned, right?" Sophie asked, her voice hushed.

"That's what the guide said," Leo replied, his attention focused on his recorder. "But this signal—it's too organized to be random. Someone's using this tunnel for something."

Sophie shivered, glancing back toward the main group. They were still within sight, the guide's flashlight bobbing as he continued his tour. "We shouldn't get too far from the others," she said. "Emma will kill us if we—"

She stopped abruptly as a faint sound echoed down the passage. It was subtle, almost imperceptible, but enough to make her freeze. A whisper. Or was it a breeze? It was impossible to tell.

"Did you hear that?" Sophie whispered.

Leo nodded, adjusting his headphones. The whispering sound wasn't loud enough for him to catch clearly, but it was there—low, almost melodic, and definitely unnatural. He pressed a button on his recorder, capturing the sound.

"This isn't interference," he said quietly. "This is... something else."

"Something else like what?" Sophie asked, her voice rising slightly. "This whole section is supposed to be abandoned."

"Exactly," Leo said, pulling his headphones down. "If it's abandoned, why would there be a signal? And why does it sound like... voices?"

Sophie didn't answer. Instead, she grabbed his arm, pulling him back toward the group. "Whatever it is, we're not finding out alone. Come on."

Reluctantly, Leo let her guide him back to the others. The guide was still talking, his voice echoing faintly off the walls as he described the construction of the tunnels during World War II. Emma turned as they rejoined the group, her eyes narrowing.

"Where were you two?" she whispered sharply.

Leo held up his recorder. "I picked up something strange. A signal—down that side tunnel."

"Seriously?" Max asked, leaning in. "What kind of signal?"

"Not interference," Leo said, keeping his voice low. "It's too regular. And there were sounds—like whispers."

Emma frowned, glancing toward the side passage Leo had indicated. It looked unremarkable, just another dark corridor lost in the maze of tunnels. But the way Leo described it made her skin prickle.

"Did the guide say anything about it?" Emma asked.

"We didn't ask," Sophie said. "But it's marked off-limits."

"Which makes it suspicious," Max said, a glint of curiosity in his eyes.

Emma sighed, glancing toward the guide, who had moved on to another part of the tunnel. "Let's not bring it up now," she said. "If it's abandoned, we can come back later and check it out ourselves."

Leo nodded, though his fingers itched to replay the recording. He glanced back at the dark passage, a flicker of movement catching his eye—but when he looked again, the corridor was empty.

For the rest of the tour, the siblings stayed close to the group, but their minds were elsewhere. The guide's rehearsed stories felt hollow compared to the possibilities hinted at by the signal Leo had captured. The abandoned section of the tunnel wasn't abandoned at all—and whatever was hidden there, they were determined to uncover it.

Chapter 4: The Map Fragment

The air grew colder as the group ventured deeper into the tunnels. The guide led the way, his flashlight illuminating the path ahead, while the Edmondsons lingered toward the back. Their earlier discovery of the strange signal still lingered in their minds, each sibling quietly mulling over what it could mean.

Ava, always keen to notice the little details others missed, slowed her pace as they passed a crumbling section of the tunnel wall. The structure was older here, the bricks uneven and coated in a thin layer of grime. The walls were marked with graffiti and scrawled symbols—some bold and colorful, others faded with age.

She stopped abruptly, her eyes catching something unusual amid the chaos of lines and colors. A small, curled piece of paper peeked out from a crack in the wall, barely visible in the dim light. It was yellowed and brittle, the edges frayed as though it had been there for decades.

"Hey, wait," Ava said, crouching down to get a better look.

The others turned to see her carefully pulling the paper from its hiding spot. It resisted slightly, but with a gentle tug, it came free. She held it up to her flashlight, revealing a faded fragment of what appeared to be a map.

"What is it?" Max asked, stepping closer.

"It's part of a map," Ava said, her voice tinged with excitement. The fragment was small, no bigger than a postcard, but it was covered in markings—cryptic symbols, faint lines, and what looked like coordinates scribbled along one edge.

"Let me see," Emma said, leaning in. She studied the map, her brow furrowing. "These symbols... they're not just random. They look deliberate, like some kind of code."

Sophie peered over her shoulder. "It's definitely old. Look at the edges—it's been here for years."

"Decades, maybe," Ava added, carefully turning the paper over. The back was blank, save for a faint watermark in the shape of interlocking gears. "This symbol looks familiar," she said, tracing the watermark with her finger.

Leo, who had been quietly observing, spoke up. "Interlocking gears. That's the same logo as the one on the guide's badge."

The siblings exchanged glances, a mix of curiosity and unease settling over them.

"Why would this map be hidden in the wall?" Sophie asked. "And why does it match the guide's logo?"

"Because it's not just a map," Emma said, her voice firm. "It's a clue. Someone left this here for a reason."

The guide's voice echoed from up ahead, snapping them out of their thoughts. "Please stay with the group," he called, his tone slightly impatient.

"Let's keep moving," Emma whispered, tucking the map fragment into her pocket. "We can figure this out later."

The siblings hurried to catch up with the group, but their focus was no longer on the guide's rehearsed stories. Ava's discovery had shifted their priorities. The fragment wasn't just a piece of old paper—it was a piece of the puzzle.

Later, as the tour wound down and the guide led the group back toward the exit, Ava couldn't resist pulling the map fragment out again. She held it close to her chest, shielding it from the others' view, but her siblings leaned in to study it more closely.

"There's something written along the bottom," Leo said, pointing to the faint text near the edge of the fragment. "It's hard to read, but it looks like... coordinates."

"Coordinates to what?" Max asked.

"Or where?" Emma added. "If this is part of a larger map, it could be pointing to something hidden in the tunnels."

"Like the door," Sophie said, her voice low. "What if this map leads to whatever's behind that door we found earlier?"

Ava's eyes lit up at the idea. "That makes sense. The map was hidden—maybe whoever left it behind wanted someone to find it, but only if they were paying attention."

"Like us," Max said with a grin. "We're good at paying attention."

Emma shot him a look. "This isn't a joke. If the guide's logo is on this map, then he might know more than he's letting on. We need to be careful."

As they reached the surface, the cool underground air gave way to the warmer bustle of Berlin above. The siblings emerged into the light, blinking against the brightness of the city. The tour had officially ended, and the guide was already moving to say goodbye to the group, but the siblings hung back, their thoughts consumed by the fragment.

Once the rest of the group had dispersed, Emma approached the guide casually, the others following close behind. "Thanks for the tour," she said, keeping her tone light. "It's an incredible network down there."

The guide nodded, his expression polite but distant. "It's a fascinating part of Berlin's history. I'm glad you enjoyed it."

"Yeah, especially all the old markings on the walls," Ava added, her voice deliberately casual. "Some of them looked really interesting—like the interlocking gears, for example."

The guide's eyes flicked toward her, his neutral expression slipping for just a moment. "Yes," he said slowly. "The gears are an emblem of some of the Cold War engineering projects in the tunnels. Many of the markings are remnants of that time."

"And the maps?" Ava pressed. "Were they part of those projects too?"

The guide hesitated, his gaze narrowing slightly. "There are many fragments of maps down there," he said, his tone carefully controlled. "Most of them are incomplete and have no real significance."

Emma stepped in, her voice firm but friendly. "So if someone found a map fragment, it wouldn't be important?"

The guide's eyes lingered on her for a long moment before he smiled faintly. "It would depend on the map."

Without another word, he turned and walked away, leaving the siblings standing in silence.

"That was suspicious," Max said as they watched him disappear into the crowd.

"Very suspicious," Ava agreed, clutching the fragment tightly. "He knows something. I could see it in his face."

Emma nodded. "And now we know we're onto something. We just need to figure out what."

As they headed back to their hotel, the siblings couldn't help but feel a growing sense of urgency. The map fragment wasn't just a piece of Berlin's history—it was a clue to something bigger, something hidden beneath the city. And they were determined to uncover it.

Chapter 5: The Missing Tour Guide

The siblings woke early the next morning, their minds still buzzing with questions about the previous day's discoveries. Ava's map fragment had been studied from every angle, its cryptic symbols and faint coordinates sparking endless speculation. They were convinced it was tied to the hidden door and the whispers Leo had picked up in the tunnels. If anyone had answers, it was the guide.

"We have to talk to him again," Emma said as they gathered in their hotel room. "He knows something, and we need to find out what."

"Agreed," Max said, stretching. "But let's not forget he seemed pretty uncomfortable when we brought up the map yesterday. If we push too hard, he might shut us down completely."

"I think he's already hiding something," Sophie said, tying her shoes. "Why else would he act so weird about the door and the symbols? He's definitely holding back."

"We'll approach him carefully," Emma said, pulling her jacket on. "No accusations, no pressure. We'll act like we're just curious tourists."

Leo smirked, his camera hanging around his neck. "Yeah, because we're so good at acting normal."

The siblings returned to the same underground tour office where they had met the guide the previous day. It was a modest space tucked into the corner of an old building, marked only by a small sign reading Berlin Underground Exploration. Inside, the air smelled faintly of old books and damp stone. A young woman sat at the front desk, typing on an ancient-looking computer.

Emma approached her with a friendly smile. "Hi, we were on yesterday's tour with Erich. We were hoping to ask him a few follow-up questions about the tunnels."

The woman looked up, her expression polite but blank. "Erich?"

"Yes," Emma said. "The guide from yesterday. He mentioned a lot of interesting things, and we wanted to learn more."

The woman frowned, shaking her head. "There must be some mistake. We don't have a guide named Erich."

The siblings froze.

"What do you mean?" Max asked, stepping forward. "He gave us the tour yesterday. Tall guy, grey coat, German accent."

"I'm sorry," the woman said, her frown deepening. "But I've worked here for three years, and I've never heard of anyone by that name working with us."

Leo leaned on the desk, his voice sceptical. "So who was leading the tour yesterday?"

"The tours are self-guided right now," the woman said, her tone firm. "We provide audio devices and maps, but we haven't employed live guides since the start of the year."

The siblings exchanged confused glances. Sophie opened her mouth to argue but stopped when Emma placed a hand on her arm.

"Thank you," Emma said to the woman, her voice calm. "That's helpful."

The woman nodded, clearly eager to return to her work. The siblings stepped outside, the brisk morning air cutting through their confusion.

"Okay, what is going on?" Sophie demanded. "We were on a tour. With a guide. Are we just supposed to believe he doesn't exist?"

"Maybe she's lying," Max said, glancing back at the building. "Covering for him."

"Or maybe he's not really part of the company," Leo said, his mind racing. "If he's working outside their system, he wouldn't show up in their records."

"Which means he has his own agenda," Emma said, her tone grim. "And we walked right into it."

The mystery deepened as they made their way back to the tunnels. They hoped to catch Erich before the next group of tourists arrived, but when they reached the entrance, there was no sign of him. The siblings waited for nearly an hour, scanning every passerby, but the guide never appeared.

"He's not coming," Ava said finally, clutching her sketchbook. "He's gone."

"Why would he disappear?" Sophie asked, pacing. "It's like he knew we were onto something."

"Or someone else was onto him," Max said darkly. "What if we weren't the only ones asking questions?"

Emma glanced at the entrance to the tunnels, her mind working through the possibilities. "If Erich was hiding something about the door and the map, he might've gotten scared. Or he might've been trying to protect us."

Leo looked sceptical. "From what?"

"From whatever's really down there," Emma said. She pulled the map fragment from her pocket, holding it up for the others to see. "This is the key. Whatever's behind that door, this map leads to it. And Erich knew it."

Determined to find answers, the siblings decided to retrace their steps from the tour. They navigated the familiar passages of the underground network, their flashlights casting long shadows on the graffiti-covered walls. The tunnels were eerily quiet, their footsteps echoing faintly.

As they approached the section where the hidden door had been, a sense of unease settled over them. The door was still there, its outline faint beneath the layers of graffiti, but something had changed.

"There," Ava said, pointing to the base of the door. "That wasn't there yesterday."

The others followed her gaze. A faint smudge of dirt on the floor, as though the door had been opened and then closed again. The edges of the frame looked cleaner, too, as though someone had disturbed the grime.

"Someone's been here," Max said, his voice low. "Recently."

"Do you think it was Erich?" Sophie asked.

"Or someone else," Emma said. "Someone who knows what's behind this door."

Leo pulled out his recorder, checking for any unusual signals. Almost immediately, the same rhythmic bursts from the previous day flickered across the screen. He adjusted the settings, his expression tightening as the bursts grew louder.

"It's stronger today," he said. "Whatever's sending this signal—it's active."

"Which means we're not alone down here," Emma said.

The siblings exchanged nervous glances, their curiosity now mingled with a growing sense of caution. Erich's sudden disappearance, the strange map, the door, and now the signal—they were all pieces of a puzzle, and the siblings were determined to solve it.

But as they stood in the damp, shadowy tunnel, a single thought echoed in Emma's mind: If Erich left, was it because of what he found—or because of who else is looking for it?

Chapter 6: The Secret in the Café

The siblings emerged from the tunnels into the crisp Berlin afternoon, their minds racing with unanswered questions. Erich's disappearance and the mystery surrounding the hidden door left them restless. They had decided to regroup and think through their next steps, and a cozy café across from the tunnel entrance seemed like the perfect spot.

The café was small and charming, with wooden tables, mismatched chairs, and walls covered in vintage posters. The scent of freshly brewed coffee mingled with the faint tang of cinnamon, providing a momentary comfort from the weight of their adventure.

Emma led the way to a corner table by the window, where they could keep an eye on the street outside. Ava immediately pulled out the map fragment, spreading it carefully on the table. Leo set up his recorder, hoping to analyse the signal again later.

"What do we know so far?" Emma asked, breaking the silence. "Let's lay it all out."

"First, the map," Ava said, pointing to the faded symbols. "It's old—probably from the Cold War era. The interlocking gears logo ties it to something mechanical or industrial, maybe even military."

"And the door," Max added. "It's clearly connected. Someone's been using it recently, and it's definitely hiding something."

"Then there's the signal," Leo said, gesturing to his recorder. "It's not random. It's structured, like it's transmitting data. But who or what is sending it?"

"And don't forget Erich," Sophie said, sipping her hot chocolate. "Whoever he is, he's gone now. Either he's avoiding us, or someone made him disappear."

The group fell silent for a moment, the weight of their discoveries settling over them. Emma was about to speak when a figure approached their table.

The café owner was a wiry man in his sixties, his apron smudged with flour. He carried a tray of drinks, which he set down with surprising grace. "Coffee for you," he said, his voice tinged with a thick German accent. "Hot chocolate for the young lady. And for you, tea."

"Thank you," Emma said, startled. "But we didn't—"

"Order?" The man smiled knowingly, his grey eyes twinkling. "No, you didn't. But I couldn't help overhearing your discussion about the tunnels. You looked like you could use something warm while you talk."

The siblings exchanged nervous glances but thanked him anyway. The man lingered, his gaze drifting to the map fragment on the table.

"That," he said softly, "is older than it looks. Dangerous, too."

Emma tensed. "What do you mean?"

The man straightened, glancing around the café as though to ensure they weren't overheard. "Many things were hidden in the tunnels during the Cold War. Secrets, weapons, technology—things better left untouched."

"You're saying this map is connected to those secrets?" Ava asked, her voice filled with curiosity.

The man's gaze lingered on the fragment. "Perhaps. Maps like this were used to mark locations—places no one was supposed to find. If you have one, it means someone trusted you—or wanted you to find what they left behind."

"But what's behind those places?" Leo pressed. "We've already seen signs of activity down there. Someone's using those tunnels now."

The man's expression darkened. "Not everyone respects history. Some seek to profit from it."

The siblings leaned in closer, their attention fixed on the café owner. "Do you know what's behind the door we found?" Max asked. "The one sealed with graffiti?"

"Ah," the man said, a flicker of recognition crossing his face. "The graffiti hides much. That particular door... I've heard whispers. They say it leads to an old bunker, one of many. But that one is... special."

"Special how?" Emma asked, her voice firm.

"It was used during the Cold War to store experimental technology," the man explained, lowering his voice. "Prototypes. Inventions designed to give one side an advantage over the other. Some say those who worked on it vanished when the project ended."

"Vanished?" Sophie repeated, her tone sceptical. "Like Erich?"

The man tilted his head. "Perhaps. The tunnels have a way of swallowing people. But if he disappeared after showing you this map, you must be cautious. There are those who would stop at nothing to keep these secrets buried."

Ava frowned, tapping her pencil against the table. "If this technology was so important, why leave it behind?"

The man shrugged. "The Cold War ended, but not all its shadows disappeared. Perhaps they thought it was safer hidden. Or perhaps it was abandoned because it was too dangerous."

"Dangerous how?" Leo asked, his curiosity overriding his caution.

"Power can be a curse," the man said simply. "The things hidden in those tunnels were never meant for ordinary people. If they are found by the wrong hands, the consequences could be catastrophic."

The siblings sat in silence, processing his words. Emma was the first to speak. "Do you think we should stop looking?"

The man studied her for a moment, then shook his head. "If you've already begun, the answers will find you, whether you seek them or not. But beware—every step closer will bring you further into the shadows."

The café owner straightened and gathered the empty tray. "Finish your drinks," he said, his voice lightening. "And if you value your safety, do not go alone."

As he walked away, the siblings exchanged uneasy glances. The map, the door, the signal—everything seemed to be pointing them toward something bigger than they had anticipated. And now, the stakes felt higher than ever.

"What do we do now?" Sophie asked, her voice barely above a whisper.

Emma reached for the map fragment, folding it carefully and tucking it into her jacket. "We keep going. If Erich was scared enough to disappear, it means we're on the right track. And if that bunker holds the answers, we're going to find them."

Max grinned. "Let's just hope we don't get swallowed by the tunnels first."

The group laughed nervously, their determination renewed. As they left the café, the warning echoed in their minds: The shadows of the Cold War were never meant to see the light.

Chapter 7: The Code in the Journal

The Berlin flea market was alive with activity, a kaleidoscope of colors, sounds, and the occasional shout from vendors advertising their wares. Rows of stalls stretched out in every direction, offering everything from antique clocks and vintage postcards to forgotten relics of Berlin's turbulent past. The siblings moved through the crowd, their eyes scanning the tables for anything that might connect to their growing mystery.

"This place is amazing," Ava said, sketchbook in hand as she jotted down quick outlines of interesting finds. "It's like walking through a time capsule."

"Let's focus," Emma said, her gaze darting between the vendors. "We're looking for anything that ties back to the tunnels—the map, the gears, anything Cold War related."

"You mean like this?" Max asked, holding up a rusted canteen with Cyrillic writing on it.

Sophie rolled her eyes. "I don't think that's going to help us unlock a secret bunker."

Max grinned, setting the canteen back down. "You never know."

Leo, meanwhile, had wandered ahead, drawn to a stall cluttered with old books, maps, and other paper ephemera. The vendor, an elderly woman with sharp eyes and a warm scarf wrapped around her shoulders, nodded politely as he approached.

"Anything interesting?" Emma asked, joining him.

"I'm not sure," Leo said, flipping through a stack of faded documents. "But this looks promising."

He pulled out a battered leather-bound journal, its cover cracked with age. The corners were worn, and a faint smell of mildew clung to the pages. As he flipped it open, the siblings crowded around him.

The pages were filled with cramped handwriting, strange diagrams, and what looked like schematics. But what caught their attention immediately was a series of symbols scattered throughout the journal—symbols that matched the ones on Ava's map fragment.

"Look at this," Ava said, her voice rising with excitement as she pointed to a page. "These spirals and marks—they're exactly like the ones on the map!"

"And here," Leo added, pointing to a different section. "This text is in German, but these numbers look like coordinates."

Emma turned to the vendor, holding up the journal. "Where did you get this?"

The woman shrugged. "A clearance sale. It came with a box of old papers and maps. Most of it was junk, but I thought this looked interesting. It's been sitting here for weeks."

"Do you know anything about who it belonged to?" Max asked.

"No," the woman replied, shaking her head. "But if you like it, I can let you have it for twenty euros."

"Done," Emma said, pulling out her wallet.

With the journal in hand, the siblings found a quiet corner of the flea market to examine it more closely. They spread it open on a table, their eyes darting over the intricate notes and drawings.

"This is more than just a journal," Leo said, his voice filled with awe. "It's a codebook."

Ava ran her fingers over one of the diagrams, tracing a series of interconnected gears. "This matches the watermark on the map fragment. Whoever wrote this had to be involved in the same project."

"Look at this page," Max said, flipping to the middle of the journal. "It's a schematic for some kind of machine."

The drawing showed a complex network of gears, pipes, and valves, with labels written in tight German script. A small box in the corner bore the same spiral symbol that appeared on the map fragment.

"What do you think it does?" Sophie asked, leaning closer.

"I have no idea," Emma admitted. "But it's connected to the tunnels—and to the door. Look at this notation." She pointed to a line of text beneath the schematic. "It mentions a 'Schlüssel'—that means 'key' in German."

"A key?" Leo said, his excitement growing. "Do you think it's referring to the Berlin Key?"

"It has to be," Ava said. "The journal, the map, the door—it's all tied together. Whatever's behind that door, this journal might tell us how to get to it."

As they flipped through the journal, Sophie stopped on a page filled with tightly written text and a series of numbers. "What about this? It looks like a cipher."

Leo peered over her shoulder, his fingers hovering above the page. "It's a substitution cipher—one of the simplest kinds. I can crack it."

He pulled out his phone, opening a decryption app he'd downloaded during one of their previous adventures. As the others watched, he entered the letters and numbers, his fingers flying over the screen.

After a few minutes, Leo let out a triumphant laugh. "Got it! It's coordinates."

"Coordinates to what?" Max asked.

"I don't know," Leo said, showing them the decoded text. "But they're not far from here."

The siblings packed up the journal and map, their minds racing with the possibilities. As they walked toward the coordinates, Emma couldn't shake the feeling that they were being watched. She glanced over her shoulder, scanning the crowd, but saw nothing out of the ordinary.

"Do you think this journal belonged to Erich?" Sophie asked as they turned onto a quieter street.

"It's possible," Emma said. "Or someone like him. Whoever wrote this knew about the tunnels and the secrets hidden down there. And now, so do we."

"But why leave it at a flea market?" Ava wondered aloud. "If it's so important, why wasn't it hidden?"

"Maybe they were trying to get rid of it," Max suggested. "Or maybe they wanted someone to find it."

Emma nodded, her expression serious. "Either way, we've got the pieces. Now we just have to figure out how they fit together."

As they reached the coordinates, the siblings stopped, staring at the building in front of them. It was an unassuming brick structure, its façade cracked and weathered. A faded sign above the door read Werkstatt für historische Restauration—Workshop for Historical Restoration.

"It doesn't look like much," Max said, tilting his head. "But we've learned not to trust appearances."

Emma nodded, gripping the journal tightly. "Let's find out what's inside."

With that, the siblings pushed open the door, stepping into the next chapter of their mystery.

Chapter 8: Shadows in the Underground

The air in the tunnels felt heavier than before, thick with dampness and the faint metallic tang of rusted machinery. The siblings moved cautiously, their footsteps echoing faintly off the narrow walls. The dim beams of their flashlights cut through the darkness, illuminating graffiti-covered concrete and tangled wires overhead.

They had returned to the underground network to retrace their steps. Armed with the journal and the map fragment, they hoped to make sense of the strange connections they had uncovered so far. But the tunnels seemed different this time—quieter, darker, as if the shadows themselves were pressing closer.

"I don't remember it being this creepy last time," Sophie muttered, her voice low.

"It's the silence," Leo said, adjusting his recorder. "Feels like the tunnels are holding their breath."

"Stop trying to freak us out," Max said, though his nervous glance over his shoulder betrayed his bravado.

Emma led the way, clutching the journal tightly under her arm. "Let's focus," she said. "We need to find the door again and see if the journal gives us any clues about how to open it."

The group walked in tense silence, the faint scuff of their shoes the only sound in the vast expanse of the tunnels. But as they turned a corner, Ava suddenly stopped, her hand shooting up in a silent signal.

"Wait," she whispered. "Did you hear that?"

The others froze, their flashlights swaying slightly. Emma listened carefully, her ears straining against the oppressive quiet. At first, there was nothing. Then, faintly, she heard it: the soft crunch of footsteps on gravel—echoing from somewhere behind them.

"Someone's there," Ava said, her voice barely audible.

Emma nodded, motioning for the group to turn off their flashlights. One by one, the beams went dark, plunging them into near-total darkness. Only the faint, flickering light from a distant fixture illuminated the tunnel ahead.

They crouched low, pressing themselves against the cold, damp wall, straining to hear. The footsteps grew louder, more deliberate, echoing ominously through the empty space. Whoever it was, they weren't trying to hide their approach.

"Do you think it's Erich?" Sophie whispered, her breath warm against Emma's ear.

"I don't know," Emma replied, her voice tense. "But whoever it is, they're following us."

The footsteps paused. The silence stretched, heavy and suffocating, and then a new sound emerged—soft, metallic, like the scrape of a tool against concrete. Emma felt her heart thudding in her chest as she tried to piece together what the noise could mean.

"We need to move," Leo whispered, his hand gripping his recorder tightly. "We're sitting ducks here."

Emma nodded, motioning for the group to stay low as they crept forward, their steps as quiet as possible. They turned down a side passage, the tunnel narrowing around them. The further they went, the more the sounds of their follower faded—but the unease remained.

"Do you think we lost them?" Max asked, his voice barely above a whisper.

"Maybe," Emma said, glancing back. "But keep moving."

The siblings navigated through a series of branching tunnels, the journal's map and the symbols on the walls guiding their path. Every so often, Emma glanced over her shoulder, half-expecting to see a shadowy figure emerging from the darkness. But the tunnel remained empty, the faint hum of electricity overhead their only companion.

Finally, they reached the section of the tunnel where the hidden door was located. The graffiti-covered metal frame was just as they had left it, its edges slightly cleaner than the surrounding wall—a telltale sign that someone had disturbed it recently.

"There it is," Ava said, relief and apprehension mingling in her voice. "Now what?"

"Let's see if the journal has anything useful," Emma said, flipping it open. She turned to the pages marked with spirals and gears, running her finger over the notes. "This symbol here," she said, pointing to a series of interlocking circles. "It's the same as the watermark on the map fragment."

"Do you think it's a key?" Sophie asked.

"Not exactly," Leo said, squinting at the diagram. "It looks more like a locking mechanism—something mechanical."

"Like a puzzle," Ava said, crouching near the door. "Look at this." She pointed to a small, rusted indentation near the base of the frame. "This matches the shape in the journal."

Emma knelt beside her, holding the journal up for comparison. The two shapes were nearly identical. "It's a slot," Emma said. "But for what?"

Before they could investigate further, the sound of footsteps returned—closer this time, and faster. The siblings froze, their eyes darting toward the tunnel from which they had come.

"They're back," Max said, his voice low and urgent.

"Whoever it is, they're not friendly," Sophie added.

Emma stood, gripping the journal tightly. "We need to hide. Now."

They quickly scanned the area, spotting a dark alcove carved into the tunnel wall a few meters away. Without a word, they darted toward it, squeezing into the cramped space. The shadows swallowed them as they pressed themselves against the cold stone, their breathing shallow and quiet.

The footsteps grew louder, accompanied by the faint beam of a flashlight cutting through the darkness. The siblings held their breath as the light swept past their hiding spot, illuminating the area near the hidden door.

A figure stepped into view, tall and clad in dark clothing. They moved with purpose, their flashlight aimed directly at the door. In their other hand, they held a metal tool—a crowbar or something similar.

"Who is that?" Sophie mouthed, her eyes wide.

Emma shook her head, her heart pounding as she watched the figure examine the door. The person muttered something under their breath, too faint to hear, before jamming the tool into the door's frame. The sound of metal scraping against metal echoed through the tunnel.

"They're trying to open it," Leo whispered, clutching his recorder.

The siblings stayed silent, their fear mingling with frustration. They were so close to uncovering the door's secrets, but whoever this was had beaten them to it.

Suddenly, the figure stopped, their flashlight flickering briefly. They froze, glancing over their shoulder as if sensing they were being watched. For a tense moment, the siblings feared they had been discovered.

But then, as abruptly as they had appeared, the figure withdrew the tool and stepped back from the door. They turned, disappearing into the darkness with hurried steps.

The siblings waited in silence, their breaths shallow, until the footsteps faded completely. Only then did Emma dare to speak.

"They're gone," she said, her voice barely audible. "But they'll be back."

"Who do you think they were?" Max asked, stepping cautiously out of the alcove.

"Someone who knows what's behind that door," Ava said, her expression grim. "And they want it just as much as we do."

Emma turned to the group, her jaw set with determination. "Then we need to figure this out before they do. Whoever they are, they're not going to stop—and neither are we."

Chapter 9: The Cold War Connection

The siblings returned to their hotel room, adrenaline still coursing through their veins after the unsettling encounter in the tunnels. Emma paced near the small desk, flipping through the journal while Leo replayed the audio recordings on his laptop. The others gathered around, their eyes darting between the journal and the growing pile of notes they had assembled from their adventure so far.

"There's something we're missing," Emma muttered, scanning the dense writing in the journal. "Whoever wrote this, they weren't just documenting random tunnels. They were tracking something—planning something."

"And whoever that was in the tunnels tonight," Max said, leaning back on the bed, "they know exactly what they're after."

"What if they're part of the same project?" Sophie suggested. "Maybe this isn't just about one door or one map. What if it's all connected?"

"Connected to what, though?" Ava asked, sketching the spiral symbols in her notebook. "What could be so important that people are still chasing it decades later?"

Emma paused, her finger tracing a section of the journal. "This," she said, pointing to a phrase scrawled in cramped handwriting. It was underlined multiple times, accompanied by a rough sketch of interconnected tunnels. The German text read: Versteck der Operation Elysium.

"'Versteck' means 'hideout' or 'cache,'" Emma translated, her excitement growing. "And 'Operation Elysium'—it has to be a codename for something."

Leo turned his laptop toward her, typing the phrase into a translation app. "If it's a codename, it might be in the declassified Cold War archives," he said. "The government's released a ton of documents in the past few years."

"And if it hasn't been declassified?" Max asked.

"Then we dig deeper," Emma said. "This journal is a breadcrumb trail. If we follow it, we'll find the answers."

They spent the next hour scouring online archives and historical databases, cross-referencing the journal's notes with known Cold War operations in Berlin. Finally, Leo struck gold. "Got something," he said, spinning his laptop to show the group. "Operation Elysium. It's mentioned in a declassified CIA document from 1991."

The others crowded around, their eyes scanning the document on the screen. The text was partially redacted, with thick black lines obscuring key details, but enough remained to give them a glimpse into the operation.

"'Operation Elysium,'" Emma read aloud, "'was a joint effort between Western intelligence agencies to develop strategic defences during the height of the Cold War. Central to the operation was a hidden bunker beneath Berlin, designed to house experimental technology.'"

"Experimental technology?" Ava echoed. "What kind of technology?"

"Doesn't say," Leo replied, scrolling through the document. "But it mentions the bunker was connected to the underground tunnel network. It was supposed to be self-sustaining, with its own power supply and communication system."

"And let me guess," Max said, leaning closer, "the bunker wasn't on any official maps."

"Of course not," Emma said. "This was top-secret. If anyone outside the operation found it, it could've jeopardized everything."

Sophie frowned, crossing her arms. "So, let's recap. There's a hidden bunker somewhere in the tunnels, tied to Cold War experiments. We've got a map fragment that might lead to it, a journal full of cryptic notes, and someone else who's clearly after the same thing."

"And we still don't know what's behind that door," Max added.

"Not yet," Emma said. "But this gives us context. If that door leads to the bunker—and I think it does—then what's behind it isn't just history. It's something valuable. Something people would kill to protect or control."

Leo nodded, his expression serious. "The document said the bunker was abandoned after the Cold War ended. But if someone's using it now…"

"Then whatever's in there didn't stay abandoned," Emma finished. She leaned back, her thoughts racing. "We need more information."

The next day, the siblings decided to visit a small Cold War museum they had passed earlier in their trip. It was housed in a nondescript building on the outskirts of Berlin, its collection focused on the city's divided history and the shadowy operations that had taken place beneath its streets.

The museum was quiet, with only a few other visitors wandering through the exhibits. The siblings split up, each scanning the displays for anything that might tie to the tunnels or Operation Elysium.

Emma paused in front of a glass case containing old maps of Berlin's underground network. Most were marked with the locations of known bunkers and escape routes, but one map caught her eye. It was labelled Tunnels of Strategic Interest and included several redacted sections where information had been deliberately removed.

"That looks familiar," Max said, joining her. He pointed to a section of the map that roughly matched the area where they had found the hidden door. "There's our neighbourhood."

"And it's blacked out," Emma said. "Whatever was there, they didn't want anyone to find it."

A museum curator, an older woman with sharp eyes and a welcoming smile, approached them. "You have an interest in the tunnels?" she asked in lightly accented English.

Emma nodded. "We've been exploring the underground network. There's so much history down there."

"There is indeed," the curator said, her gaze lingering on the map. "And much of it is still hidden. During the Cold War, both sides buried secrets in Berlin's underground—some of which have yet to be uncovered."

"Like Operation Elysium?" Emma asked, watching for a reaction.

The curator's smile faltered slightly. "That is a name I have not heard in a long time," she said carefully. "But yes, I imagine it is connected."

"Do you know what the operation was about?" Max asked.

The curator hesitated, then nodded. "It was said to involve advanced technology—prototypes that could give one side an advantage in the arms race. But the operation was abandoned after reunification, and much of its documentation was destroyed or sealed."

"Do you think any of it is still down there?" Emma pressed.

The curator's eyes narrowed slightly. "If it is, I would advise you to be cautious. Those tunnels have been quiet for years, but not everyone respects their history. There are those who seek profit, not understanding."

The siblings exchanged uneasy glances, her words echoing their encounter in the tunnels.

As they left the museum, Emma clutched a photocopy of the map she had requested from the curator. The redacted sections loomed large in her mind, their secrets tantalizingly close yet frustratingly out of reach.

"This just confirms it," she said as they walked back toward the hotel. "That door leads to something tied to Operation Elysium. We're not just chasing a mystery—we're chasing a piece of Cold War history that someone wants to keep hidden."

"And we're not the only ones chasing it," Sophie reminded her.

Emma nodded, her determination hardening. "Then we need to get there first. Whatever's behind that door, it's part of a bigger story. And we're going to find out what it is."

Chapter 10: The Puzzle Room

The air in the tunnels was cooler than before, the musty scent of damp stone and rust lingering as the siblings ventured deeper into the network. They were armed with the journal, Ava's map fragment, and a new determination after uncovering the bunker's connection to Operation Elysium. Guided by faint markings on the walls that matched the symbols in the journal, they pressed on, their flashlights cutting through the darkness.

"Are you sure we're going the right way?" Sophie asked, glancing nervously at the narrowing passage ahead.

Emma nodded, holding the journal in one hand and her flashlight in the other. "The symbols are all here," she said, pointing to a faint spiral etched into the wall. "We're following the right trail."

"It better lead somewhere," Max muttered, his voice echoing faintly. "Preferably not to a dead end."

Ava, walking near the back, stopped suddenly. "Wait," she said, shining her flashlight on the ground. "Do you see that?"

The others turned, their beams converging on a faint, uneven track on the floor—a groove worn into the stone, as though something heavy had been dragged through the passage.

"It's recent," Leo said, crouching to examine the track. "Look at the edges. It hasn't been worn down over time."

"Someone's been here," Emma said, her voice low. "And not that long ago."

The siblings followed the groove until the passage widened into a small chamber. The walls were lined with rusted pipes and cracked tiles, remnants of the Cold War infrastructure that had once run through the tunnels. But what caught their attention immediately was the array of objects scattered across the floor and walls.

In the center of the room stood a large, broken piece of machinery, its gears and levers frozen in place by years of rust. Diagrams were pinned to the walls, their edges curling and yellowed with age. And at the back of the room, partially hidden by debris, was a heavy metal safe, its door sealed tight.

"This place is incredible," Ava whispered, pulling out her sketchbook. She immediately began to draw the broken machine, her pencil capturing the intricate details of its design.

"What is all this stuff?" Max asked, stepping closer to the machinery. He reached out to touch one of the levers, only for it to crumble slightly under his fingers. "It's like something out of a science fiction movie."

Emma flipped through the journal, her brow furrowed. "This machine—it's in here," she said, holding up a page that depicted a rough sketch of interconnected gears and valves. "But the notes don't explain what it's for."

Leo was already examining the diagrams on the walls. "These look like schematics," he said, his voice tinged with excitement. "But they're incomplete. Like someone started designing something and then abandoned it."

"Or they didn't want anyone to know what they were building," Sophie said, her gaze fixed on the heavy safe at the back of the room. "That thing, though—that's not abandoned."

The others turned to see what she was pointing at. The safe was massive, its surface scarred with scratches and dents, as though someone had tried—and failed—to force it open. A large dial lock was mounted at its center, along with a small keypad that looked strangely modern compared to the rest of the room.

"Who leaves a safe like this in the middle of a bunker?" Max asked, stepping closer.

"Someone who doesn't want anyone to get inside," Emma said. She crouched in front of the safe, studying the lock and keypad. "This doesn't match the rest of the room. It's newer."

"Do you think it's connected to Operation Elysium?" Leo asked.

Emma nodded slowly. "If this is the bunker they used for experimental technology, whatever's in this safe could be what they were working on."

The siblings spent the next hour exploring the room, piecing together what they could from the diagrams, machinery, and notes. Ava carefully documented everything in her sketchbook, while Leo snapped photos of the diagrams to analyse later. Max and Sophie examined the machine, trying to determine if any of its parts were still functional.

"This lever moves," Max said, gripping a rusted handle and pulling it downward. A faint creak echoed through the room, but nothing else happened. "Or... maybe not."

Sophie rolled her eyes. "Great job, mechanic."

Meanwhile, Emma focused on the journal, flipping back and forth between pages as she tried to decipher the notes. Her flashlight flickered, casting shifting shadows across the walls.

"There's something here," she muttered, pointing to a passage written in dense German text. "It mentions a 'Hauptschlüssel'—a master key. I think it's talking about the safe."

"Does it say how to open it?" Max asked.

Emma scanned the text again, her eyes narrowing. "Not directly. But it describes a sequence—something about aligning gears and inputting a code."

Leo perked up at the mention of a code. "Do you think it's related to the cipher we cracked earlier? The coordinates?"

"It's possible," Emma said. "If the coordinates led us here, the code could be the next step."

They gathered around the safe, their flashlights trained on the keypad and dial. Emma held the journal open, her finger tracing the sequence described in the text. "Okay," she said, taking a deep breath. "If I'm reading this right, we need to align the dials to match the schematic."

Ava flipped to her sketch of the machine. "The gears are supposed to form a spiral," she said, holding up the page. "Like this."

Max adjusted the dials, turning them slowly until they mirrored the pattern in Ava's drawing. The room was silent except for the faint clicks of the mechanism.

"Now the code," Emma said, stepping forward. She entered the numbers they had deciphered from the journal—4-9-2-7-6—into the keypad.

For a moment, nothing happened. Then, a faint beep echoed through the room, and the safe's lock clicked audibly.

"It worked," Sophie whispered.

Emma gripped the safe's handle and pulled. The door creaked open, revealing a small, dimly lit compartment inside. The siblings leaned in, their breaths catching as they saw what lay within: a metal case, no larger than a briefcase, stamped with the same interlocking gears emblem they had seen on the map.

"What do you think is in it?" Ava asked, her voice barely audible.

"We're about to find out," Emma said, reaching for the case.

As she lifted it from the safe, a faint hum filled the air, growing louder with each passing second. The siblings exchanged uneasy glances as the sound reverberated through the room.

"Uh... is that supposed to happen?" Max asked, stepping back.

Emma set the case down carefully, her heart pounding. "I don't think so," she said. "But whatever this is, it's not staying here."

As the hum intensified, the siblings knew they had to move quickly. The room, the machine, the diagrams—everything pointed to something far bigger than they had imagined. And now, they had the key to unlocking it.

Chapter 11: A Hidden Enemy

The siblings made their way cautiously back through the tunnels, the metal case clutched tightly in Emma's hands. The faint hum they'd heard in the puzzle room still echoed in their minds, a strange and unsettling sound that hinted at the case's mysterious contents. But the weight of what they'd discovered wasn't the only thing on their minds.

They weren't alone in the tunnels.

Ava was the first to notice. As they turned a corner, her flashlight caught the faintest flicker of movement up ahead—a shadow that darted out of sight too quickly to be natural. She froze, her hand shooting up to signal the others.

"Wait," she whispered. "Did you see that?"

The group stopped, their flashlights scanning the tunnel ahead. The air felt heavier, and the faint echo of voices reached their ears—a low murmur coming from further down the passage.

"Someone's there," Leo said quietly. He adjusted his recorder, hoping to pick up the conversation.

Emma motioned for them to stay close, her grip tightening on the case. The siblings crept forward, their footsteps as quiet as they could manage. The voices grew louder, clearer, until they could make out distinct words.

"They said the Berlin Key is in one of the hidden rooms," a man's voice said, low and gruff. "We just have to keep searching."

"And what if it's not?" another voice replied, this one higher and sharper. "We've been chasing these tunnels for weeks, and we still don't know what we're looking for."

"Don't be stupid," the first voice shot back. "The Berlin Key is real. You saw the documents—Operation Elysium, the experiments, all of it. The treasure's here, and the key will lead us to it."

The siblings exchanged nervous glances, their curiosity piqued. Emma leaned closer to the wall, trying to catch more of the conversation. Whoever these people were, they weren't casual explorers—they were after something specific.

"And the safe?" a third voice chimed in. "If someone else finds it first?"

"Then we take it from them," the gruff man replied. "No one else knows what they're looking for. They're just stumbling around in the dark. But we've got the advantage."

The voices began to move, their echoes growing fainter as the group of treasure hunters disappeared down another passage. The siblings stayed frozen in place until the last echoes of footsteps faded entirely.

"What was that about?" Sophie whispered, her voice tense. "The Berlin Key? What is it?"

Emma shook her head. "I don't know, but it sounds like it's important. They think it's tied to Operation Elysium—and to something they're calling 'the treasure.'"

"But what treasure?" Max asked, glancing nervously down the tunnel. "We haven't seen anything that looks like treasure."

"Whatever it is, it's worth enough for them to keep searching," Ava said. "And for them to threaten anyone who gets in their way."

Leo adjusted his camera, his expression grim. "We've got to figure out what this Berlin Key is—and fast. If they're looking for the same thing we are, we don't have much time."

The siblings hurried back toward the surface, their minds racing. The mention of the Berlin Key had introduced a new layer of mystery, one that seemed to connect everything they'd uncovered so far: the map, the journal, the bunker, and now the metal case. But it also brought a new danger. Whoever those treasure hunters were, they weren't afraid to use force to get what they wanted.

As they climbed the steps to the street above, Emma glanced back at the case in her hands. "We need to find a safe place to figure this out," she said. "And we need to research the Berlin Key. If it's tied to Operation Elysium, it could explain everything."

"Do you think those guys know about the case?" Sophie asked, her voice edged with worry.

"They don't know we have it," Emma said. "At least, not yet."

"But they will," Max added. "Especially if we're heading toward the same goal."

Emma nodded, her jaw set with determination. "Then we'll get there first. Whatever the Berlin Key is, we'll figure it out—and we'll make sure it doesn't fall into the wrong hands."

As they stepped into the bustling Berlin streets, the shadows of the tunnels still seemed to cling to them. The treasure hunters weren't just rivals—they were a looming threat. And the mystery of the Berlin Key had only just begun.

Chapter 12: The Key's Blueprint

The siblings sat at a long wooden table in the quiet corner of Berlin's State Library, the towering shelves of books stretching above them like walls of knowledge. The air smelled faintly of old paper and polished wood, and the distant hum of activity was muffled in the sprawling reading room.

Emma set the metal case on the table, her fingers brushing its cool surface. They hadn't dared open it yet, wary of what might lie inside. Instead, they had decided to focus on researching the Berlin Key, hoping to unravel its significance before risking whatever secrets the case held.

Ava had already pulled a stack of books on Cold War history, her pencil poised to jot down anything useful. Max flipped through a dusty archive of maps, while Sophie scrolled through digitized records on a library tablet. Leo worked on translating passages from the journal using an online tool.

"We know it's tied to Operation Elysium," Emma said, scanning the notes they had gathered so far. "And we know it's important enough that those treasure hunters are after it. But what does it do?"

"Maybe it's the key to the safe," Max suggested. "Or to whatever's behind the hidden door."

"Or maybe it's something bigger," Ava said, flipping through a book on Cold War cryptography. "The word 'key' doesn't have to mean a literal key. It could mean anything—an idea, a system, even a cipher."

Emma looked up sharply. "A cipher?"

Ava nodded. "Think about it. If Operation Elysium was about experimental technology, they wouldn't use a simple lock and key to secure it. They'd use something more advanced."

Leo perked up, tapping on his laptop. "I just found something. There's a mention of the Berlin Key in an old cryptography journal." He angled the screen so the others could see. "It describes it as a 'conceptual tool' designed to unlock secure systems."

"What kind of systems?" Sophie asked, leaning closer.

Leo scanned the text. "It says the key was part of a dual-encryption mechanism. Half of it was a physical object—a device or a machine. The other half was a cipher, like a code you'd need to decode the data the device produced."

"So it's not just a key," Emma said slowly. "It's a system."

"Exactly," Leo said. "The physical part unlocks something tangible, like a safe or a door. But the cipher unlocks the information inside."

"That would explain why those treasure hunters are so desperate to find it," Ava said. "If the Berlin Key can access secure systems, it could hold the answers to everything Operation Elysium was working on."

Max pulled out the map fragment they had found earlier, tracing the symbols with his finger. "If the Berlin Key is a cipher, could the map be part of it?"

"It's possible," Ava said. "The spirals and symbols could be coordinates, or a way to align the mechanism."

"And the journal has plenty of coded notes," Leo added. "They might make sense once we understand how the cipher works."

"But we still don't know what the physical key is," Sophie pointed out. "Or where to find it."

Emma thought for a moment, her gaze fixed on the metal case. "What if we already have it?"

The others fell silent, their eyes turning to the case. It was heavy, solid, and stamped with the interlocking gears emblem tied to Operation Elysium. They had been hesitant to open it without more information, but now it seemed like the logical next step.

"Do we do it here?" Max asked, glancing around the library.

"No," Emma said firmly. "If the Berlin Key is as important as we think, we can't risk anyone seeing it. We'll take it back to the hotel."

They continued their research, diving deeper into the cryptography journal and historical records. A pattern began to emerge: mentions of the Berlin Key as a critical piece of Cold War strategy, references to hidden systems buried beneath Berlin, and hints that the key's true purpose was more than just defence.

"It's like they were trying to build something revolutionary," Ava said, sketching out a diagram from one of the books. "Something that could change the balance of power."

"But they abandoned it," Sophie said. "Why?"

"Maybe it was too dangerous," Emma said. "Or maybe they didn't have time to finish it before the Cold War ended."

Leo nodded. "Whatever the reason, it's still down there. And the Berlin Key is the only way to unlock it."

As the library lights dimmed, signalling the end of the day, the siblings packed up their notes and carefully wrapped the case in a cloth to conceal it. They left with a renewed sense of purpose—and a creeping sense of urgency. The Berlin Key wasn't just a relic of the past; it was a blueprint for something far more significant. And they weren't the only ones who knew it.

As they stepped into the cool evening air, Emma glanced over her shoulder, half-expecting to see shadows trailing them. The treasure hunters were out there, and they were closing in.

But the Edmondsons were ready. They had a piece of the puzzle—and they weren't giving it up without a fight.

Chapter 13: The Mysterious Benefactor

The siblings returned to their hotel room with their newfound knowledge about the Berlin Key, their minds racing with possibilities. The metal case sat on the desk, unopened, as though daring them to uncover its secrets. Emma was about to suggest they open it when a knock at the door interrupted their thoughts.

Max exchanged a wary glance with Emma. "Were we expecting anyone?"

"No," Emma replied, moving cautiously to the door. She peered through the peephole and saw a man standing in the hallway, clutching an oversized satchel. His appearance was striking: a long tweed coat, a bowtie slightly askew, and wiry grey hair that looked as though he'd run his hands through it repeatedly. His thick glasses reflected the hallway light, making his expression unreadable.

"Who is it?" Sophie asked, moving closer.

"No idea," Emma said, opening the door just enough to speak. "Can I help you?"

The man smiled warmly. "Ah, you must be Emma Edmondson. You and your siblings have been making quite the waves. May I come in? I believe we have much to discuss."

The siblings hesitated but ultimately allowed the man into the room. He introduced himself as Dr. Victor Klein, a historian specializing in Cold War secrets and underground operations.

"How did you find us?" Leo asked, his suspicion evident.

"I have my sources," Dr. Klein replied with a dismissive wave. "The better question is how you stumbled upon the Berlin Key. That particular artifact has eluded some of the finest minds for decades."

The siblings exchanged uneasy glances. Ava finally spoke. "We're just… curious travellers. We've been exploring the tunnels and piecing things together as we go."

Dr. Klein chuckled. "Please. Don't insult my intelligence. The map, the journal, the case—you've found fragments of one of the greatest Cold War mysteries. And I want to help."

"Why would you want to help us?" Emma asked, crossing her arms.

"Because," Dr. Klein said, leaning forward, "the Berlin Key isn't just a piece of history—it's the key to a technological marvel that could reshape how we understand the Cold War, and perhaps even the present."

Dr. Klein began pulling documents from his satchel, spreading them across the desk. Old photos, faded blueprints, and heavily redacted government files painted a fragmented picture of Operation Elysium.

"These tunnels you've been exploring were part of a vast underground network used for experimentation," Dr. Klein explained. "The Berlin Key was central to their work—a cipher and device designed to unlock a system known as the 'Elysium Core.'"

"What's the Elysium Core?" Sophie asked.

"A self-sustaining energy source," Dr. Klein said, his voice dropping to a near whisper. "If the reports are true, it was decades ahead of its time. Clean energy, infinite scalability—a true revolution. But it was abandoned as the Cold War drew to a close."

"Why abandon something so powerful?" Max asked.

"Fear," Dr. Klein said. "Fear that it could fall into the wrong hands. Fear that it wasn't stable. The Core and its access points were sealed, and the Berlin Key vanished—until now."

Emma glanced at the case. "And you think we've found part of the key?"

"I do," Dr. Klein said, his gaze fixed on the case. "And I can help you unlock its potential. But only if we work together."

"What do you mean?" Leo asked.

"Share your discoveries with me," Dr. Klein said. "The journal, the case, any maps or clues you've found. In return, I'll help you navigate the dangers ahead. And believe me, there are dangers."

The siblings exchanged uneasy glances. "What kind of dangers?" Emma asked.

Dr. Klein sighed, pulling out a grainy photo of men in dark coats standing near a tunnel entrance. "You're not the only ones looking for the Berlin Key. There are others—treasure hunters, yes, but also those with far more nefarious intentions. If they find the Core first... let's just say the consequences would be catastrophic."

"Why should we trust you?" Sophie asked. "For all we know, you could be working with them."

Dr. Klein smiled faintly. "You're right to be cautious. But think about it: if I wanted the key for myself, I wouldn't have come to you. I'd have let those hunters take it off your hands. No, I want to see this discovery preserved, not exploited."

The room fell silent as the siblings considered his words. Finally, Emma spoke. "We'll think about it. But for now, we're keeping the case."

"Of course," Dr. Klein said, standing and gathering his papers. "Take your time. But don't take too long. The deeper you go, the more dangerous this becomes. And without guidance, you may not survive."

As he reached the door, he turned back, his gaze sharp. "One last piece of advice: watch your backs. The Berlin Key isn't just a mystery—it's a magnet. And it's already attracting attention."

With that, he was gone, leaving the siblings in a tense silence. They had more questions than ever, but one thing was clear: the Berlin Key was far more than they had imagined—and their discovery had placed them in the crosshairs of something much bigger than themselves.

Chapter 14: The Safe's Secret

The next day, the siblings returned to the puzzle room in the tunnels. Armed with the knowledge they had gleaned from their research—and a growing sense of urgency—they were determined to uncover more of the secrets hidden in the depths of Berlin.

The room looked just as they had left it, a jumble of rusted machinery, faded diagrams, and the unassuming heavy safe that had so far kept its contents locked away. But something felt different. The air seemed charged, almost expectant, as if the room itself was waiting for them to uncover its secrets.

Emma stood in front of the safe, her hand on the dial. "The journal mentioned a second locking mechanism," she said, flipping to a page filled with sketches and cryptic annotations. "The first safe was straightforward, but this one... it's more complicated."

"Complicated how?" Max asked, crossing his arms.

"Look at this," Emma said, pointing to a drawing in the journal. "The dial isn't just for numbers. It's a puzzle. The journal says you have to align specific symbols in a sequence to open it."

Leo crouched beside her, studying the dial. "Symbols? Like the ones on the map fragment?"

"Exactly," Emma said. "The spirals and gears—they're part of the code."

The siblings worked together, comparing the map fragment and the journal to the safe's dial. Ava sketched the sequence on a scrap of paper, her pencil moving quickly as she translated the spirals into a series of movements.

"Okay," she said after a few minutes. "I think we've got it. Turn the dial clockwise to the first spiral, counterclockwise to the second, and then back to the third."

Emma took a deep breath, gripping the dial. "Here goes."

The others watched in tense silence as she carefully turned the dial, following Ava's instructions. The clicks of the mechanism echoed in the still room, each sound heightening their anticipation. When Emma completed the sequence, she pulled on the handle.

At first, nothing happened. Then, with a loud clunk, the lock disengaged.

"You did it!" Sophie said, her voice breaking the silence.

Emma pulled the safe's door open, revealing its contents: a reel of film in a metal canister, wrapped in paper, and several brittle sheets of parchment folded neatly beneath it. The siblings crowded around, their excitement mingling with curiosity.

"What's this?" Max asked, carefully lifting the reel. The label was faded, but a few words were still legible: Elysium Project—Confidential.

"It's film," Leo said, inspecting it. "Probably from the Cold War. If it's labelled 'confidential,' it has to be important."

"And these?" Ava asked, unfolding the parchment. The brittle sheets were covered in intricate drawings and symbols—more maps, similar to the fragment they had found earlier.

"These are detailed," Emma said, tracing one of the lines with her finger. "They show parts of the tunnel network we haven't seen yet. Look—this one has a red 'X.' It's marking something."

"A treasure?" Max asked, leaning closer.

"Or the Core," Sophie suggested. "If these maps are part of the Berlin Key, the red 'X' could show where it's hidden."

Emma turned her attention back to the film reel. "If the maps show us where to go, the film might tell us why. We need to find a projector."

"Do you think Dr. Klein could help?" Leo asked.

Emma hesitated. "Maybe. But if we bring him into this, we're trusting him with everything. Are we ready for that?"

"We don't have much of a choice," Ava said. "We don't know what's on this film or what we're walking into. If Klein has more information, we might need him."

Emma nodded reluctantly. "Then let's get this stuff out of here and figure out our next move."

The siblings carefully packed the film reel and the maps into their bag, their minds racing with possibilities. The safe had given them new pieces of the puzzle, but it had also raised more questions. What was on the film? What was the red 'X' marking on the map? And how much danger were they stepping into by following the trail of the Berlin Key?

As they left the puzzle room and retraced their steps through the tunnels, Emma glanced over her shoulder, half-expecting to see shadows trailing them. The thought of the treasure hunters and their mysterious goals sent a chill down her spine.

Whatever was waiting for them at the end of the map, it wasn't just a piece of history. It was something far bigger—and far more dangerous. And they were about to find out just how far they would go to uncover the truth.

Chapter 15: The Midnight Encounter

The hotel room was quiet, the siblings finally asleep after a long day of decoding symbols, tracing maps, and debating their next steps. The safe's contents—the film reel and additional map fragments—were tucked away in Emma's travel bag, carefully concealed beneath layers of clothes. The journal lay on the desk, next to Ava's sketchbook, its pages marked with sticky notes and scrawled annotations.

Outside, the city hummed softly with late-night life. A distant train rumbled, and the occasional laughter of passing tourists filtered through the partially open window. It was the kind of calm that felt almost impenetrable.

Until it wasn't.

Emma stirred in her sleep, her ears pricking at a faint noise she couldn't quite place. At first, she thought it was part of a dream—the creak of the door, the soft rustle of fabric—but then a distinct click reached her ears. Her eyes snapped open, her heart pounding. The room was dark, but the faintest sliver of light from the hallway illuminated a shadow moving near the desk.

She sat up silently, her mind racing. Someone was in their room.

She glanced at the others, still asleep in their respective beds, their breathing steady and undisturbed. Carefully, Emma slid off the bed, her movements slow and deliberate. She reached for her phone on the nightstand, but her hand froze as the figure turned, their silhouette briefly outlined against the window. Whoever it was, they were rifling through the journal.

Emma's breath caught as she realized what they were after. The map fragments and journal—everything they had uncovered so far—were at risk of being stolen. She needed to act fast. Without a sound, she crept toward Max's bed, shaking his shoulder gently.

"Max," she whispered, her voice barely audible. "Wake up."

Max groaned softly, blinking blearily. "What...?"

"Shh!" Emma hissed. "Someone's here."

That snapped him awake. His eyes widened as he registered her words, and he turned his head toward the desk. The figure was still there, their back to the siblings as they leafed through the journal.

Max's gaze darted around the room, landing on a heavy glass water bottle on the table by the window. He grabbed it, nodding to Emma, who motioned for him to stay quiet. Together, they moved closer, their steps soundless against the carpeted floor.

Just as they were within arm's reach, the intruder froze, as if sensing their presence. They spun around, their hooded face obscured in the dim light. Without hesitation, they lunged toward the window, clutching the journal in one hand.

"Stop them!" Emma shouted, her voice waking the others.

Max hurled the water bottle, narrowly missing the intruder but startling them enough to stumble. Sophie and Leo were up in an instant, their shouts filling the room as the figure scrambled to climb out the window onto the fire escape.

Emma darted toward the desk, grabbing the map fragments and shoving them into her bag. "They've got the journal!" she yelled, her adrenaline surging.

Leo ran to the window, looking down at the fire escape. The intruder was already descending, their movements quick and practiced. "They're getting away!"

"Not for long," Max said, bolting for the door. "I'm going after them."

The siblings raced after Max, their bare feet slapping against the cold hallway floor as they followed him down the stairs. The sound of the fire escape clanging below spurred them on, their determination outweighing their fear.

When they burst out into the alley behind the hotel, the intruder was already at the far end, darting into the shadows of a side street.

"Split up!" Emma shouted. "Cut them off!"

Max and Sophie veered left, while Emma, Leo, and Ava took the right. The siblings sprinted through the narrow streets, their eyes scanning the darkness for any sign of movement. The faint echo of running footsteps guided them as they pushed themselves harder, their breaths ragged.

Emma caught a glimpse of the figure ahead, their hood slipping briefly to reveal short, dark hair. She shouted, her voice ringing out in the empty street. "Stop! We know what you're after!"

The intruder didn't stop. Instead, they turned sharply into a narrow alley, disappearing around the corner. When the siblings reached the same spot, the alley was empty—just a row of trash bins and a single flickering streetlight.

"They're gone," Sophie said, her hands on her knees as she caught her breath. "Did anyone see their face?"

Emma shook her head, frustration boiling inside her. "No. But they were after the journal—and they got it."

The siblings regrouped back in their hotel room, their exhaustion replaced by a simmering determination. The desk was a mess, the open window still letting in the cool night air. Emma picked up the water bottle Max had thrown, setting it back on the table.

"We still have the map fragments and the case," Leo said, trying to sound optimistic. "The journal was important, but we can work without it."

"But the journal had so much information," Ava said, her voice heavy with worry. "What if they use it to find the Berlin Key before we do?"

Emma set her jaw, her eyes burning with resolve. "Then we work harder. We still have the maps, the film reel, and everything we've learned so far. Whoever they were, they think they've got the upper hand. But they don't know who they're up against."

The siblings nodded, their bond stronger than ever despite the loss. They didn't know who had broken into their room or why, but one thing was certain: the race for the Berlin Key was heating up, and the stakes had never been higher.

Chapter 16: The Film in the Bunker

The siblings sat in tense silence, the metal film canister resting on the table between them like a relic of some forgotten age. After the events of the previous night—the break-in, the loss of the journal—they had redoubled their efforts to uncover the truth behind the Berlin Key. Their only hope now lay with the reel of film they had retrieved from the safe.

Emma glanced at her siblings. "We need to play this," she said firmly. "Whatever's on it could be the key to understanding Operation Elysium—and what we're up against."

"But where?" Ava asked. "We can't exactly waltz into a movie theatre and ask them to play it."

Leo had been scrolling through his phone, his brow furrowed. "There's an old projector in one of the side tunnels," he said, holding up a photo from an article about abandoned Cold War infrastructure. "It's part of an underground bunker used during the Cold War. If it still works, we can use it to play the film."

Max raised an eyebrow. "You're suggesting we drag this reel back into the tunnels where we just got chased by treasure hunters?"

Emma nodded. "We don't have a choice. If this reel holds the answers, we need to see it."

The siblings made their way into the tunnels, their flashlights cutting through the heavy darkness. The air was colder than usual, carrying the faint metallic tang they had come to associate with the underground. Leo led the way, his phone's GPS guiding them to the location of the bunker.

When they reached the entrance, it was clear the bunker hadn't been used in decades. The heavy metal door hung slightly ajar, its surface streaked with rust. Inside, the siblings found a small room cluttered with abandoned equipment—filing cabinets, broken radios, and a hulking, dust-covered projector mounted on a metal table.

"This is it," Leo said, brushing off the projector. "Let's hope it still works."

Emma carefully removed the reel from its canister and handed it to Leo, who threaded the film through the projector's spools with practiced precision. Max found a switch near the back of the machine, and with a metallic groan, the projector whirred to life. A beam of light flickered onto the far wall, casting ghostly shapes across the room.

The siblings sat on the floor as the film began to play. At first, the screen was filled with static and scratches, the images faint and unsteady. Then, a title card appeared: "Operation Elysium: Strategic Infrastructure Development, 1963."

"This is it," Emma whispered, her heart pounding.

The film transitioned to grainy black-and-white footage of men in lab coats standing around a massive machine. The narrator's voice crackled through the projector's speaker, his clipped, official tone echoing in the bunker.

"Operation Elysium," the narrator began, "was conceived during the height of the Cold War as a defensive measure against potential attacks on Western Europe. Utilizing Berlin's extensive underground network, the operation aimed to create secure escape routes and hidden infrastructure for high-priority personnel."

The footage shifted to show detailed schematics of the tunnel system, overlaid with red lines marking escape routes and supply depots. One section was circled in bold red ink, labelled "Elysium Core."

"That's the same name Dr. Klein mentioned," Sophie said, leaning forward. "The Elysium Core."

The film continued, showing workers installing machinery in a cavernous underground chamber. The narrator explained that the Elysium Core was an experimental energy system designed to power the bunker network indefinitely.

"The Core," the narrator said, "utilizes advanced principles of energy generation, providing a sustainable and secure power source for emergency operations. However, concerns about its stability and potential misuse have resulted in its classification as highly restricted."

The footage became more ominous, showing soldiers guarding the Core and locking away blueprints in secure safes. The narrator's tone shifted, tinged with urgency.

"To prevent the Core from falling into enemy hands, access is controlled through the Berlin Key: a dual-encryption mechanism requiring both physical and cryptographic components. Without both, the Core cannot be activated."

The film ended abruptly, the final frame freezing on a grainy image of a massive steel door labelled "Elysium Core Access." The siblings sat in stunned silence as the projector whirred to a halt, the room plunging into darkness except for the dim glow of their flashlights.

"That explains the Berlin Key," Ava said finally, her voice trembling with excitement. "It's the only way to access the Core."

"And the treasure hunters think they can use it," Emma said, her mind racing. "If they get to the Core, they could reactivate it—or worse, weaponize it."

"But why abandon it?" Max asked. "If the Core was so important, why not use it?"

"Because it wasn't stable," Leo said, repeating the narrator's words. "They were afraid of what it could do."

Emma stood, her resolve hardening. "We need to find the Core before anyone else does. The maps and fragments we have—they're leading us to it."

"But what if it's dangerous?" Sophie asked, her voice laced with worry. "What if we're walking into something we can't control?"

Emma met her gaze, her expression determined. "We didn't choose this, but we're the only ones who can stop the wrong people from getting there first. If we don't act, no one will."

The siblings packed up the reel and maps, their purpose clearer than ever. The tunnels still held secrets, and at their heart lay the Elysium Core—a Cold War relic that could either be humanity's salvation or its undoing.

As they stepped back into the dark passageways, Emma glanced at the flickering light of the projector one last time. The past was no longer buried, and the stakes had never been higher.

Chapter 17: The Network's True Purpose

The siblings trudged through the damp, shadowy tunnels, the hum of the film's projector still echoing in their minds. The revelation about the Elysium Core had been shocking enough, but there had been something else in the narrator's voice—an unspoken implication that the underground network wasn't just about escape routes or energy solutions. It was about something more.

"What do you think the narrator meant when he said the network had a 'restricted secondary function'?" Ava asked, her sketchbook clutched tightly under her arm.

"Something dangerous," Emma said, her voice grim. "The way they talked about the Core—it wasn't just an energy source. It was a weapon."

"But how?" Sophie asked, her flashlight beam flicking across the tunnel walls. "It sounded like it was supposed to help people, not hurt them."

"That's what they said publicly," Leo said, pulling out his phone to recheck the notes he had made from the film. "But if the Core was unstable, it might have had side effects they didn't expect—or they realized it could be weaponized."

As they continued deeper into the tunnel system, their conversation was cut short by a new discovery. Leo stopped abruptly, his flashlight illuminating a junction where several tunnels branched out in different directions. On the wall ahead was a faded map, partially torn but still legible. Several sections were marked with numbers and symbols.

"Look at this," Leo said, stepping closer. "This map is older than the ones we've seen so far. It's like a blueprint for the whole network."

Emma scanned the map, her eyes narrowing as she traced one of the red lines. "These aren't just escape routes," she said. "They're access points—control stations."

"For what?" Max asked, leaning over her shoulder.

"Look at this symbol," Ava said, pointing to a spiral icon near one of the marked areas. "It matches the ones on the journal and the map fragments."

Emma's finger stopped on a section of the map labelled Zone Theta. Unlike the other areas, which were labelled with practical terms like "Supply Depot" or "Medical Bay," Zone Theta was circled in red and marked with a warning: AUTHORIZED PERSONNEL ONLY—EXTREME CAUTION.

"What's Zone Theta?" Sophie asked, her voice tinged with unease.

"It's got to be one of the 'secondary functions' the narrator mentioned," Emma said. "Whatever's there, it's dangerous enough to warrant this kind of warning."

Leo pulled out his phone and snapped a photo of the map. "We need to find this zone. If the Core is connected to it, we need to know what it's capable of."

As they continued down the passageway, the tunnels grew narrower and more cluttered with debris. Pipes jutted out from the walls at odd angles, and the faint smell of oil and mildew lingered in the air. The siblings stayed close, their flashlights flickering across the walls as they searched for signs of Zone Theta.

After what felt like an eternity, they reached a large, circular chamber. The room was filled with rusted machinery and stacks of abandoned crates, many of them stencilled with faded symbols. One crate bore the words CLASSIFIED MATERIALS—DO NOT OPEN.

"This has to be part of it," Max said, brushing dust off the lettering. "They didn't leave warnings like this for nothing."

Emma opened one of the crates carefully, her breath catching as she uncovered a pile of old documents and blueprints. The papers were brittle, their edges curling with age, but the symbols and diagrams were unmistakable. One page showed a schematic of the Core, its intricate machinery surrounded by annotations in German.

"These are detailed plans for the Core," she said, holding up one of the blueprints. "But look at this."

She pointed to a section of the blueprint labelled Emergency Containment Protocols. The accompanying notes described a mechanism designed to isolate and neutralize the Core in the event of a catastrophic failure.

"They were afraid of it," Leo said, reading over her shoulder. "They didn't just abandon the project—they were trying to contain it."

As they sifted through the documents, Ava found a weathered logbook tucked inside another crate. Its entries were written in hurried, almost frantic handwriting.

"Listen to this," Ava said, translating the German text aloud. "'Test 47: Energy output exceeded safe levels. Containment protocols engaged. Potential for widespread damage—recommend suspension of further trials.'"

"Widespread damage?" Sophie repeated, her voice rising. "They knew it was unstable and kept testing it?"

"Not just unstable," Ava said, flipping to another entry. "'Test 51: Unauthorized personnel detected near Zone Theta. Security breach reported. Orders issued to secure all access points immediately.'"

The siblings exchanged uneasy glances.

Emma's gaze shifted to a metal panel embedded in the wall near the back of the chamber. Unlike the other equipment, it was polished and intact, its surface marked with the same interlocking gears emblem they had seen on the map and journal. Above the panel was a red warning light, long extinguished but still foreboding.

"This isn't just a bunker," Emma said, her voice steady but tense. "This is a control center—for something much bigger."

"What do you think it controls?" Max asked, stepping closer.

Emma studied the panel, her mind racing. "I don't know. But if the Core is tied to Zone Theta, and this network was built to support it..."

"Then the network wasn't just for escape routes," Leo finished. "It was for control—and containment."

As they left the chamber, the weight of their discovery settled over them. The Berlin underground wasn't just a relic of the past; it was a system designed to hold something dangerous, something that had been left buried for a reason.

But now, it wasn't just history. It was their responsibility.

As they navigated the twisting tunnels, Emma glanced at the map fragments they had pieced together. Their path was clear: Zone Theta was the next step. And with each step, the stakes grew higher. The Core wasn't just a piece of forgotten technology—it was a ticking time bomb waiting to be unearthed.

Chapter 18: The Stranger's Warning

The siblings emerged from the tunnels into the fading evening light, their minds still racing with everything they had uncovered. They had returned to the surface to regroup, the weight of their discoveries pressing heavily on them. The blueprints, the logs, and the warnings about the Core all pointed to one undeniable truth: they were dealing with something far beyond what they had expected.

"Let's grab some food and figure out our next move," Emma said, tucking the map fragments carefully into her bag. "We need to decide how to approach Zone Theta."

"Assuming we're not walking into a death trap," Sophie muttered, though she followed without argument.

They found a small café near a quiet park, its outdoor seating surrounded by string lights and ivy-covered trellises. The siblings settled at a corner table, their conversation hushed as they poured over their notes and sketches. Leo was in the middle of describing a possible route to Zone Theta when a shadow fell across their table.

"Excuse me," an unfamiliar voice said.

The siblings looked up to see an elderly man standing nearby, leaning heavily on a wooden cane. He was thin and wiry, his sharp blue eyes contrasting starkly with the deep lines etched into his face. His clothing was simple—a wool coat and flat cap that had seen better days—but his presence radiated an air of quiet authority.

"I couldn't help but overhear," the man continued, gesturing to their spread of maps and papers. "You're interested in the tunnels, yes?"

Emma straightened, her instincts immediately on high alert. "Who's asking?"

The man smiled faintly. "Someone who knows what lies beneath this city. And someone who knows the dangers of digging too deep."

The man pulled out a chair without waiting for an invitation, sitting down with a groan. He set his cane against the table and glanced at their maps, his expression darkening. "Zone Theta," he murmured, his fingers brushing one of the sketches. "You've found its name, then. That's further than most."

Emma exchanged a wary glance with her siblings. "You know about it?"

The man nodded slowly. "I was part of it, a long time ago. During the Cold War, I worked as an engineer on the tunnel systems—back when the network was being expanded for... unconventional purposes."

"Operation Elysium?" Leo asked, leaning forward.

The man's sharp eyes flicked to him. "You've done your homework. Yes, Elysium. The Core, Zone Theta, all of it."

"Then you know what's down there," Max said. "Why was it abandoned?"

The man sighed, his fingers tightening around the edge of the table. "Because it became too dangerous. The Core wasn't just unstable—it was unpredictable. The energy it generated was unlike anything we had ever seen, and we didn't fully understand how to control it. There were... accidents."

"Accidents?" Ava asked hesitantly.

"Power surges," the man said grimly. "Failures in the containment systems. We lost people—good people. The Core's potential was limitless, but so were its risks. And when the Cold War ended, the government decided it wasn't worth the cost. They sealed the Core and buried the project."

Emma frowned, her mind racing. "Then why not destroy it?"

The man shook his head. "We couldn't. The Core is... unique. Too valuable, too dangerous. They hoped burying it would be enough."

"But it wasn't," Leo said, his voice tinged with frustration. "People are still looking for it. Treasure hunters, historians, anyone who thinks they can use it."

"Which is why I'm here," the man said, his voice dropping. "I've seen what happens when people get too close to the Core. It consumes them—whether through greed, curiosity, or desperation. Some doors should remain closed."

The siblings fell silent, the weight of his words settling over them. For a moment, even Emma hesitated, her resolve shaken. "What are you saying?" she asked finally.

"I'm saying you should walk away," the man said, his gaze piercing. "The Core isn't a treasure. It's a Pandora's box. Whatever you hope to find, it's not worth the risk."

"But what about the people who do find it?" Sophie asked. "If we stop looking, they won't."

The man's jaw tightened, his expression unreadable. "That's the eternal problem, isn't it? But the deeper you go, the harder it will be to turn back. And the more you uncover, the more danger you'll bring upon yourselves."

Emma leaned forward, her voice steady. "We've already found too much to stop now. If the Core is as dangerous as you say, then leaving it for someone else to exploit isn't an option. We have to see this through."

The man studied her for a long moment, his blue eyes searching hers. Finally, he nodded, a flicker of respect crossing his face. "You're stubborn. I suppose I was once, too."

He reached into his coat pocket and pulled out a small, folded piece of paper. "If you're set on continuing, take this. It's an old access point—one of the few not marked on official maps. It'll get you closer to Zone Theta without drawing too much attention."

Emma accepted the paper, her fingers brushing his as she took it. "Thank you," she said quietly.

"Don't thank me yet," the man said, standing slowly and picking up his cane. "Just remember: the Core isn't something you can control. It's something you survive."

As the man disappeared into the night, the siblings sat in silence, the folded paper resting in the center of the table like a challenge. Finally, Max broke the silence.

"Well," he said, his voice shaky but resolute. "Guess we're not walking away, are we?"

Emma shook her head, unfolding the paper to reveal a crude hand-drawn map with a single word scrawled in the corner: Theta.

"No," she said. "We're not."

Chapter 19: The Treasure Hunters' Plan

The siblings crouched in the shadow of a crumbling wall deep in the tunnels, their breaths barely audible as they strained to hear the voices echoing through the passageway. The dim light from a distant flashlight cast shifting shadows on the walls, amplifying the tension in the air. Somewhere just ahead, the rival treasure hunters were having an intense discussion, their words bouncing off the stone with a sharp, conspiratorial edge.

Emma motioned for her siblings to stay quiet, her heart pounding as she leaned forward to catch the conversation. The treasure hunters had been trailing them for days, their intentions as clear as their greed. Now, it seemed, they were making their move.

"Zone Theta is the key," one voice said, low and gravelly. It belonged to the group's leader, a man they had heard referred to as Carter. "The map confirms it, and the journal we took spells out how to get in."

Max clenched his fists, anger flaring in his chest. "They stole the journal," he whispered. "That's how they're ahead of us."

"Shh," Emma warned, her focus fixed on the voices.

Another voice joined in, higher and impatient. "But the main entrance is sealed. You saw the door—it's practically welded shut."

"That's what the explosives are for," Carter replied, his tone cold and decisive. "We're not leaving without the Core."

Explosives. The word sent a chill through Emma. She turned to her siblings, her whisper barely audible. "They're planning to blow their way in."

A third voice, quieter but nervous, chimed in. "You really think this Core is worth all this trouble? The last time anyone touched it, half the facility went dark. And those containment protocols—"

"Are ancient history," Carter interrupted. "The Core is the treasure of a lifetime. Power, money, leverage—whatever you want, it's all there. We just need to get to it first."

"And what if those kids show up again?" another voice asked, this one gruff and irritated. "They're nosy, and they've been sniffing around."

"Then we deal with them," Carter said flatly. "Permanently."

Sophie's eyes widened, her breath catching. "They're talking about us," she mouthed.

Emma's jaw tightened. She motioned for her siblings to retreat, carefully backing away from the wall. The treasure hunters' voices faded as the siblings moved further into the shadows, their footsteps as silent as possible on the damp stone floor.

When they were far enough away, Emma whispered, "We need to stop them."

"How?" Max asked, his voice laced with frustration. "They have the journal, they're ahead of us, and now they have explosives."

"And they're willing to hurt us to get what they want," Sophie added, her fear barely contained.

"That just means we need to be smarter," Emma said. "They're rushing in without understanding the dangers. The Core isn't just a treasure—it's a trap. If they try to breach Zone Theta with explosives, they could set off a chain reaction."

"So what's the plan?" Leo asked.

Emma's eyes narrowed with determination. "We follow them, but we don't engage. We figure out how they're getting in, and then we find another way. If we can get to the Core first, we can stop them from using it."

"And if we can't?" Ava asked quietly.

Emma's voice was firm. "Then we make sure no one does."

The siblings moved swiftly but carefully, retracing their steps until they were back in a safe section of the tunnels. They found a quiet alcove to regroup, their minds racing as they pieced together everything they had overheard.

"We have two problems," Leo said, sketching out a rough map on a piece of paper. "One: they're planning to use explosives to breach the main entrance to Zone Theta. Two: they're armed and won't hesitate to stop us."

"And three," Ava added, "we don't have the journal anymore. Whatever clues were in there, they have them."

Emma nodded, her mind working rapidly. "But we still have the map fragments and the film reel. We know Zone Theta better than they do, even without the journal."

"And we have the old man's map," Sophie pointed out. "The one that shows the hidden access point."

Emma unfolded the hand-drawn map the stranger had given them, her finger tracing the route to Zone Theta. "This might be our advantage. If they're using the main entrance, we can use this to get around them."

The siblings spent the next hour planning their next move, mapping out the best way to reach Zone Theta without being detected. Every step they took had to be calculated, every decision precise. The treasure hunters were ahead of them, but the siblings had something they didn't: an understanding of the stakes.

"This isn't just about getting there first," Emma said as they packed up their gear. "It's about protecting what's down there. If they get to the Core, they won't just take it—they'll use it."

"And if we can't stop them?" Max asked, his voice heavy.

Emma's gaze was steady. "Then we make sure the Core never leaves Zone Theta."

With their plan in place, the siblings set off into the tunnels once more, their resolve stronger than ever. The treasure hunters had a head start, but the Edmondsons had something more valuable: each other.

And they were ready to do whatever it took to stop the Core from falling into the wrong hands.

Chapter 20: The Map Complete

The siblings sat cross-legged on the floor of their makeshift base in the tunnels, a dim flashlight illuminating the papers, sketches, and fragments spread before them. Ava, her brow furrowed in concentration, carefully arranged the map pieces like a puzzle, each fragment offering another piece of the larger picture.

"This has to fit here," she muttered, sliding one fragment next to another. "And this one… connects to that spiral marking."

Emma leaned closer, her eyes scanning the symbols Ava had pieced together. "It's starting to make sense," she said. "Look—these markings align with the tunnel schematics we found in the blueprint."

"And this area," Leo pointed out, tracing a section with his finger, "matches the red circle on the film reel map. That has to be Zone Theta."

Ava nodded, her hands steady despite the excitement building around her. "Exactly. These fragments weren't random—they were part of a larger map showing the entire network. But more importantly, they're pointing to something specific."

She reached for the largest fragment, the one with the interlocking spiral symbol they had seen throughout their journey. Placing it at the center, she used a pencil to connect the lines across the fragments. Slowly but surely, a clear image emerged: a complete map of the Berlin underground, with a hidden bunker marked prominently near the edge of Zone Theta.

"Here," Ava said, tapping the map with her pencil. "This is it. The bunker isn't just near Zone Theta—it's built into it."

Max whistled low. "You're saying we've been circling the Core this whole time?"

"Not exactly," Ava said. "Zone Theta is massive, but this bunker seems to be its nerve center. If the Core is anywhere, it's there."

Emma studied the map, her expression serious. "This hidden bunker—it's isolated for a reason. Whatever's inside, they didn't want anyone finding it."

"But we did," Sophie said, a small smile tugging at her lips. "And we have the map to prove it."

As the siblings examined the reconstructed map, they noticed something else. Along the edges of the bunker, faint symbols and notations were scribbled in German. Leo squinted at the text, his phone's translation app ready.

"It says... 'Primary Access Sealed' and 'Secondary Access Functional,'" he read aloud. "Looks like the main entrance to the bunker is locked down."

"Just like the treasure hunters said," Max added. "That's why they're using explosives."

"But this secondary access," Emma said, pointing to a small mark near the bunker. "That could be our way in. If the treasure hunters don't know about it, we can beat them there."

The siblings worked quickly, transferring Ava's reconstructed map onto a single sheet of paper for easier reference. The route to the secondary access point wasn't straightforward, but it was manageable with the information they now had.

"We'll have to bypass a few blocked tunnels," Ava said, marking detours on the map. "But if we stick to this path, we'll reach the bunker before they do."

"And then what?" Sophie asked. "What happens when we get to the Core?"

Emma's gaze was steady. "We secure it. If it's as dangerous as everyone says, we make sure no one can use it—not the treasure hunters, not anyone."

Leo looked up from the map, his expression thoughtful. "And if it's already active?"

"Then we figure out how to shut it down," Emma said. "We've come this far—we're not turning back now."

As they packed their gear and prepared to set off, Ava carefully folded the completed map and tucked it into her sketchbook. "This map isn't just a guide," she said softly. "It's proof. Proof that the Core is real—and that we found it."

Emma smiled, placing a hand on her shoulder. "And proof that we did it together."

The siblings set off into the tunnels once more, their path clear and their resolve unshaken. The map was complete, the bunker within reach. But as the shadows of the tunnels closed around them, they knew the hardest part of their journey was still to come.

Zone Theta and the secrets of the Core awaited, and with them, the fate of the Berlin underground—and possibly much more.

Chapter 21: The Chase Underground

The air in the tunnels was heavy and still, the faint scent of mildew clinging to the damp stone walls. The siblings moved quickly but cautiously, their flashlights casting shifting beams of light ahead. The completed map Ava had reconstructed was their lifeline now, guiding them toward the hidden bunker and the secrets of Zone Theta.

But they weren't alone.

Emma stopped abruptly, holding up a hand to signal silence. The others froze, their breaths barely audible. For a moment, all was quiet, save for the faint drip of water somewhere in the distance. Then, they heard it—a low murmur of voices, punctuated by the echo of footsteps.

"They're close," Emma whispered, her grip tightening on the map. "Too close."

"Do you think they know we're here?" Sophie asked, her voice barely audible.

"They wouldn't be moving this fast if they didn't," Max replied, his jaw clenched.

Emma glanced at Ava. "How far to the secondary access point?"

Ava unfolded the map, her flashlight trembling slightly. "Maybe a quarter mile, if we stick to this route."

"Then let's move," Emma said. "Quietly."

The siblings pressed on, their footsteps careful and measured. The tunnels seemed to stretch endlessly, their interconnected passages creating a labyrinth that was as disorienting as it was foreboding. The voices of the treasure hunters grew louder, closer, until it was clear they were on the same path.

"They're catching up," Leo said, his voice low but urgent. "We need to pick up the pace."

"We can't risk them hearing us," Emma said, her mind racing. "We need to lose them."

Max gestured to a side tunnel branching off to their left. "What about this? It's not on the map, but it could throw them off."

Emma hesitated, glancing at Ava. "Does it connect back to our route?"

Ava scanned the map, her brow furrowed. "It might, but there's no guarantee. It could lead to a dead end."

"We don't have time to debate," Max said, already heading toward the side tunnel. "They're right behind us."

The siblings slipped into the side tunnel, their flashlights dimmed to avoid drawing attention. The space was narrower here, the air colder and more oppressive. Pipes jutted out from the walls at odd angles, forcing them to duck and weave as they moved. The sound of their pursuers faded slightly, but the tension remained.

"Do you think they'll follow us?" Sophie asked, her voice tinged with worry.

"They might not know we took this route," Leo said. "It's a gamble."

"Let's hope it pays off," Emma muttered.

They continued through the side tunnel, their path twisting and turning in unpredictable ways. At times, the walls seemed to close in, the ceiling so low that Max had to stoop to avoid hitting his head. The siblings were just starting to think they had evaded the treasure hunters when a distant shout shattered their fragile confidence.

"They're in here!" a voice bellowed, echoing through the passage.

"Run!" Emma hissed.

The siblings broke into a sprint, their flashlights bouncing wildly as they navigated the uneven ground. The treasure hunters' voices grew louder, accompanied by the rapid thud of approaching footsteps. The tunnel twisted sharply, forcing the siblings to make split-second decisions about which direction to take.

"Left!" Ava shouted, pointing to a wider passage. "It loops back to the main route!"

They veered left, the sound of their pursuers hot on their heels. Emma's heart pounded in her chest, her mind racing as she tried to calculate their next move. If they could reach the main route, they might have a chance to outpace the treasure hunters—but only if the map was accurate.

"Faster!" Max urged, glancing over his shoulder. "They're gaining on us!"

A sudden noise—a metallic clatter—echoed behind them. Sophie glanced back and saw one of the treasure hunters stumble, tripping over a loose pipe. The delay bought them precious seconds, but the others were still closing in.

"There!" Leo shouted, pointing ahead. "The main tunnel!"

They burst into the larger passage, their flashlights illuminating the familiar markings on the walls. Ava quickly checked the map, her hands trembling as she oriented herself.

"This way!" she said, leading them toward the secondary access point.

The siblings ran as fast as they could, their breaths coming in ragged gasps. The sound of the treasure hunters faded slightly as the twists and turns of the main tunnel worked in their favour. But the danger wasn't over.

As they neared a junction, Emma noticed a faint red glow ahead—a warning light mounted on the wall. It flickered weakly, casting eerie shadows across the passage.

"What's that?" Sophie asked, slowing slightly.

"It's marking the access point," Ava said. "We're close."

"Then let's finish this," Emma said, her determination overriding her exhaustion.

They reached the access point, a heavy metal door partially concealed behind a rusted grate. Ava pulled the map from her pocket, comparing it to the markings on the wall.

"This is it," she said, her voice triumphant. "The secondary entrance to the bunker."

"But it's locked," Max said, pointing to the thick chain securing the door.

Emma glanced back down the tunnel, the faint sound of their pursuers still echoing in the distance. "Then we'll have to break it."

Leo rummaged through his bag, pulling out a multi-tool he had brought for emergencies. "I can cut the chain, but it'll take time."

"Do it," Emma said. "We'll keep watch."

As Leo worked on the chain, the others kept their flashlights trained on the tunnel behind them. The tension was palpable, each second feeling like an eternity. Finally, with a metallic snap, the chain broke, and the door creaked open.

"Go!" Leo urged.

The siblings slipped through the door, pulling it closed behind them just as the sound of footsteps grew louder. They locked the door from the inside, the heavy bolts sliding into place with a satisfying clunk.

For a moment, there was only silence. Then, the faint sound of the treasure hunters shouting in frustration reached their ears.

"We did it," Ava said, her voice shaky with relief. "We lost them."

Emma placed a hand on her shoulder, her expression a mix of exhaustion and determination. "For now. But we're not safe yet."

As they turned to face the dimly lit passage ahead, they knew their journey was far from over. The hidden bunker and the secrets of the Core awaited, and the stakes had never been higher.

Chapter 22: The Berlin Key Found

The air inside the bunker was different—thicker, colder, and strangely charged, as though the walls themselves were humming with energy. The siblings stepped cautiously into the dimly lit corridor, their flashlights flickering against the rusted metal walls. Pipes and conduits lined the ceiling, their once-shiny surfaces now dulled by decades of neglect.

"This place feels... alive," Sophie murmured, her voice barely above a whisper.

"It's probably just the air pressure," Leo said, though even he didn't sound convinced. "Old systems can do weird things."

"Let's not stick around to figure it out," Emma said, motioning for them to move forward. "We need to find the Core—and stop the treasure hunters before they catch up."

The corridor opened into a large, circular chamber. Machinery surrounded the room, hulking shapes of metal and wire silhouetted against the faint red glow of emergency lights. A heavy metal table stood in the center, covered in scattered tools, yellowed schematics, and a strange object that immediately caught Max's attention.

"Whoa," Max said, stepping closer. "What is that?"

The object was unlike anything they had seen before. It was about the size of a human hand, made of a dark, gleaming metal that seemed almost liquid in the dim light. Its intricate design was unmistakable: interlocking spirals and geometric patterns, identical to the symbols on their map.

Max reached out hesitantly, his fingers brushing the surface. The metal was cool to the touch, almost unnaturally so.

"It's a key," Ava said, her voice filled with awe. "It has to be. Look at the symbols—it matches the ones we've been following."

Max carefully picked up the key, holding it in his hands as the others gathered around. The weight of it was heavier than he expected, as though it was more than just a piece of metal.

"This thing's incredible," Max said, turning it over to examine its intricate details. "It's not just a key—it's a piece of art."

"Or a piece of technology," Leo said, leaning in for a closer look. "The spirals aren't just decorative. They look like part of a mechanism—like the key itself is part of the lock."

"What kind of lock?" Sophie asked, glancing around the room. "Do you think it opens the Core?"

"It has to," Emma said, her voice steady but tense. "The Core is the heart of this bunker, and this key is the only thing that can access it."

"But should we use it?" Ava asked, her expression conflicted. "If the Core is as dangerous as everyone says, do we really want to unlock it?"

The siblings exchanged uneasy glances. The weight of the key in Max's hands felt symbolic—like a choice they hadn't fully realized they were about to make. Emma stepped closer, her gaze fixed on the strange object.

"We don't use it yet," she said firmly. "Not until we know more. The Core isn't just a treasure—it's a responsibility. If we use the key without understanding what we're unlocking, we could make everything worse."

Max nodded, his fingers tightening around the key. "Agreed. But we can't leave it here either. If the treasure hunters find this…"

"They won't," Emma said. "We'll keep it with us until we decide what to do."

As they explored the rest of the chamber, the siblings found more clues about the bunker's purpose. Old schematics showed the layout of Zone Theta, with a large central area labelled Elysium Core Control Room. Notes scribbled in the margins warned of "unstable energy outputs" and "restricted protocols."

"This whole place was built around the Core," Leo said, scanning one of the schematics. "It's like the key isn't just for opening it—it's for controlling it."

"But why would they make it so hard to access?" Sophie asked. "If the Core was supposed to help people, why bury it behind all these layers of secrecy?"

"Because they were afraid of it," Emma said, her voice heavy. "They didn't trust it—and maybe they didn't trust themselves."

The siblings gathered near the table, the key resting in the center as they studied their findings. The sense of urgency was growing; they knew the treasure hunters wouldn't be far behind. But the discovery of the Berlin Key had changed everything. It wasn't just a tool—it was a question. A choice.

"What do we do now?" Max asked, his gaze shifting between the key and his siblings.

Emma met his eyes, her resolve clear. "We keep moving. If the Core is ahead of us, we need to reach it first. And if we can't control it..."

"Then we make sure no one can," Ava finished, her voice steady despite the weight of her words.

The siblings packed up their findings and prepared to move deeper into the bunker. The key was secured in Max's bag, its strange weight a constant reminder of what lay ahead. As they stepped into the next passage, the red glow of the emergency lights flickered ominously, casting long shadows on the walls.

The Berlin Key was in their hands, and with it, the power to unlock the heart of Zone Theta. But as they ventured further into the unknown, one question lingered in their minds: Were they unlocking the past—or unleashing the future?

Chapter 23: The Key's Power

The siblings pressed deeper into the bunker, the dim emergency lights casting eerie shadows on the walls. Every step brought them closer to the heart of Zone Theta, their unease growing with each passing moment. Max carried the Berlin Key securely in his bag, its strange weight a constant reminder of the power they now held.

The tunnel widened abruptly into a large chamber. At its center stood a massive, reinforced door, its surface engraved with the same spirals and symbols that adorned the key. The door loomed like a sentinel, daring them to approach.

"This has to be it," Emma said, her flashlight beam sweeping across the intricate designs. "The door to the archive—or maybe something even bigger."

Ava stepped closer, her eyes tracing the symbols. "Look at this pattern," she said, pointing to a circular indentation at the center of the door. "It matches the key exactly."

Max pulled the key from his bag, its dark, gleaming surface catching the faint red light. "So... we just put it in and turn it?"

Emma nodded, her voice steady but cautious. "Slowly. We don't know what's on the other side."

Max stepped up to the door, his heart pounding as he inserted the key into the indentation. It fit perfectly, the spirals aligning seamlessly with the grooves. As he began to turn it, a faint hum resonated through the room, growing louder with each click of the mechanism.

The siblings watched in tense silence as the door began to shift. With a deep, grinding sound, the massive structure slid aside, revealing a passageway shrouded in darkness. The hum faded, replaced by a low, rhythmic pulse that seemed to emanate from deep within.

"What is that?" Sophie whispered, gripping her flashlight tightly.

"Only one way to find out," Emma said, stepping forward. "Stay close."

The passage led to a vast underground chamber, its walls lined with rows of filing cabinets, shelves, and ancient computer terminals. The air was cool and dry, the faint smell of paper and dust lingering. Dim lights flickered on overhead as they entered, illuminating a space that seemed untouched for decades.

"This is it," Leo said, his voice filled with awe. "A Cold War archive."

The siblings spread out, their flashlights sweeping across the room. Ava stopped at a tall shelf filled with binders and folders, each labelled with cryptic codes. Max approached one of the computer terminals, its bulky frame a relic of another era.

"These files look official," Ava said, pulling a folder from the shelf. "Project logs, test results... it's all here."

Emma examined a nearby filing cabinet, her fingers brushing against the faded labels. "This isn't just about the Core," she said, pulling out a folder filled with maps. "It's the entire network—every access point, every hidden passage."

"Why would they keep all this down here?" Sophie asked, her voice tinged with unease. "If they abandoned the project, why not destroy it?"

"Because they didn't abandon it completely," Leo said, flipping through a binder. "This archive wasn't just for records—it was for contingency plans. If the Core ever needed to be reactivated, they'd need everything here to do it."

As they continued to explore, Max found a small console near the center of the room. Its screen flickered to life as he pressed a few buttons, revealing a menu filled with options. One entry caught his eye: Elysium Core Control Logs.

"I think I found something," Max said, motioning for the others to join him. "These are the control logs for the Core."

Emma leaned over his shoulder, her eyes scanning the screen. "Can you access them?"

Max nodded, navigating through the menu. The screen displayed a series of entries, each one detailing the Core's activation and testing phases. One entry stood out, marked with a red warning symbol: Protocol Theta-9—Emergency Containment Initiated.

"What's Protocol Theta-9?" Ava asked, peering at the screen.

"It sounds like the shutdown procedure," Leo said. "But look at the date—it was activated just before the project was sealed."

"Why?" Sophie asked. "What happened?"

Emma clicked on the entry, revealing a series of logs and notes. The text described a catastrophic power surge during one of the Core's tests, causing widespread system failures. The final note was chilling: Containment successful. Core unstable. Recommend permanent deactivation.

"This explains why they buried it," Emma said, her voice heavy. "The Core wasn't just unstable—it was dangerous. They couldn't control it, so they locked it away."

"But someone still wanted it," Max said, his jaw tightening. "Those treasure hunters think they can use it, and they're willing to blow up half the tunnels to get to it."

Emma nodded, her resolve hardening. "Then we have to stop them. This archive might have the information we need to shut the Core down for good."

And now, the Edmondsons were the only ones who could stop it.

Chapter 24: The Document Trove

The archive was vast, an underground labyrinth of knowledge buried beneath Berlin for decades. The siblings moved through the room with purpose, their flashlights scanning rows of filing cabinets, shelves, and computer terminals. Dust motes floated in the stale air, undisturbed since the Cold War's height.

"Start looking for anything about energy," Emma said, her voice steady but urgent. "The Core, the Berlin Key—anything that ties it all together."

Ava immediately headed toward a tall shelf labelled Project Elysium - Classified, pulling down binders and files. Max moved to a set of filing cabinets, rifling through folders filled with yellowed documents. Sophie and Leo worked together at one of the ancient computer terminals, navigating the archaic interface for any relevant files.

Emma found a stack of folders on a nearby table, their labels faded but legible. She opened one marked Energy Initiative - Gamma, her breath catching as she scanned the contents. Inside were technical schematics and hand-written notes describing an experimental energy source.

"It's all here," Emma called, spreading the documents on the table for the others to see. "This is what they were working on—a new form of energy, unlike anything else."

Leo peered over her shoulder. "Look at this," he said, pointing to a diagram. "This isn't just a power source—it's a self-sustaining system. They were trying to create infinite energy."

"And they built it," Max said, holding up a schematic of the Elysium Core. "But look at the warnings. These notes talk about energy spikes, instability, and containment issues. It's like they couldn't control it."

"That's why they shut it down," Ava said, flipping through another folder. "They realized it was too dangerous. But if it's still down here—"

"It is," Sophie interrupted, her voice tinged with excitement. She had found a folder marked Core Containment - Theta Access. Inside were maps and instructions for reaching a secure chamber deep within Zone Theta.

"This has to be where the Core is," Sophie said, spreading the map out on the table. "It's marked as a containment zone. They didn't destroy it—they locked it away."

As they pieced together the story, more questions emerged. Emma held up a declassified document labelled Operation Chronos - Oversight, her brow furrowing as she read the details.

"Operation Chronos?" Max asked, leaning closer. "What's that?"

"It's mentioned here," Emma said, pointing to the text. "'Chronos' was a contingency plan to use the Core as a weapon if the Cold War escalated. They were trying to harness its energy for... mass destruction."

The siblings exchanged uneasy glances.

"So the Core isn't just dangerous because it's unstable," Ava said. "It's dangerous because it's powerful."

"And someone knew it," Leo added, pulling up a document on the computer. The screen displayed a series of redacted memos, but one phrase stood out: 'The Core must remain sealed. Its potential outweighs its risks.'

As they continued sifting through the archive, Sophie found a binder labelled Berlin Network - Energy Integration Trials. The pages inside described an underground grid that connected the Core to key locations across the city.

"Listen to this," Sophie said, reading aloud. "'During initial testing, the Core was linked to Berlin's underground network, providing power to hidden facilities. Unintended surges caused blackouts and structural damage.'"

"Unintended surges," Max repeated. "That's putting it lightly. They almost brought the whole network down."

"But the fact that it's connected means it could still be active," Emma said. "If the treasure hunters find the Core and figure out how to use it, they could tap into the network again."

"Or worse," Leo said, pointing to another memo. "'Chronos assets remain dormant.' Dormant doesn't mean destroyed. What if those weaponized systems are still in place?"

The siblings gathered the most critical documents, their minds racing with possibilities. The archive had revealed the full scope of the project: the Core was more than a technological marvel. It was a Pandora's box, capable of reshaping the world—or destroying it.

"We have what we need," Emma said, tucking the files into her bag. "Maps, schematics, containment protocols. If we're going to stop this, we need to get to the Core before the treasure hunters do."

"And what do we do when we get there?" Ava asked. "Destroy it? Lock it away again?"

Emma's gaze was steady. "We'll figure it out when we get there. But one thing's for sure—no one can be allowed to use it."

As they prepared to leave the archive, a faint rumble echoed through the tunnels. The siblings froze, their eyes darting to the heavy door they had unlocked with the Berlin Key.

"Was that... an explosion?" Sophie asked, her voice barely above a whisper.

"They've started," Emma said, her stomach sinking. "The treasure hunters are trying to breach Zone Theta."

"We need to move," Max said, grabbing his bag. "Now."

The siblings exited the archive, locking the door behind them with the Berlin Key. The hum of the tunnels seemed louder now, charged with a sense of urgency. The treasure hunters were closer than ever, and the race for the Core was reaching its climax.

As they retraced their steps through the tunnels, Emma gripped the map tightly, her mind focused on the path ahead. The Core was waiting, and with it, the answer to a question that had haunted them since they first entered the underground: What price would they pay to protect the future?

Chapter 25: The False Ally

The siblings moved swiftly through the tunnels, their bags packed with the documents and maps from the archive. The sound of distant explosions spurred them onward, each step bringing them closer to Zone Theta—and the treasure hunters who were trying to breach it.

As they rounded a corner, a familiar figure appeared in the dim light ahead. Dr. Victor Klein, the eccentric historian who had offered his help days before, stood in the center of the passage, his cane planted firmly on the ground. His sharp blue eyes glinted in the flashlight beams, and a faint smile played on his lips.

"Dr. Klein?" Emma said, her voice tinged with relief. "What are you doing here?"

"I could ask you the same," he replied smoothly. "It seems you've made quite the progress. I assume you've been to the archive?"

Emma hesitated, her instincts warning her to be cautious. "We found it," she said carefully. "And we found the Berlin Key."

Dr. Klein's eyes flicked to Max, who still held the key in his bag. "Excellent," he said, his smile widening. "You've done well, better than I could have hoped."

Something about his tone made Emma's stomach twist. "What do you mean?" she asked, stepping forward.

Dr. Klein sighed, his expression shifting to one of feigned regret. "I suppose it's time to drop the pretence. You see, I've been working with the treasure hunters from the start."

The revelation hit like a blow. The siblings stared at him, their disbelief mingling with anger.

"You've been helping them?" Sophie said, her voice rising. "All this time?"

"Not helping," Dr. Klein corrected. "Guiding. They lack... subtlety, but their ambition is admirable. And now, thanks to you, we have everything we need to unlock the Core."

Emma's jaw tightened. "You used us."

"Don't take it personally," Dr. Klein said, his tone almost condescending. "You were remarkably resourceful. It's only fitting that your efforts contribute to something greater."

"Something greater?" Max shot back. "You mean letting those thugs get their hands on a weapon that could destroy everything?"

Dr. Klein chuckled softly. "You misunderstand. The Core isn't just a weapon—it's a tool, one that could reshape the world. Power like that shouldn't remain hidden. It should be harnessed."

Emma stepped forward, her voice cold. "And you think you're the one who should harness it?"

Dr. Klein raised an eyebrow. "Why not? The treasure hunters may have brute strength, but I have knowledge. Together, we can ensure the Core is used wisely."

"And by wisely, you mean for your own gain," Ava said, her tone sharp. "You're no better than they are."

Dr. Klein's smile faded, his eyes narrowing. "Perhaps," he said. "But I have something you don't—a choice. You can give me the Berlin Key now, and I'll ensure your safety. Refuse, and my associates will make this much more unpleasant."

The siblings exchanged quick glances, their minds racing. Emma stepped back, subtly positioning herself between Dr. Klein and Max, who still held the key.

"You're not getting the key," Emma said firmly. "Not now, not ever."

Dr. Klein sighed, his expression one of theatrical disappointment. "I was afraid you'd say that."

At his signal, the sound of footsteps echoed through the tunnel. From the shadows behind him, several treasure hunters emerged, their faces hard and their weapons visible.

"Now," Dr. Klein said, his voice cool and commanding, "shall we renegotiate?"

The siblings' hearts pounded as the treasure hunters advanced. Emma's mind raced, searching for a way out. She locked eyes with Max, then glanced subtly toward a side tunnel just behind him. He caught her meaning immediately.

"Fine," Emma said, raising her hands in mock surrender. "You win. We'll give you the key."

Dr. Klein's smile returned, triumphant. "A wise decision."

Emma stepped back, her movements deliberate as she motioned for Max to hand over the key. But as he reached into his bag, he suddenly bolted for the side tunnel, clutching the key tightly.

"Run!" Emma shouted.

The siblings scattered, sprinting down different tunnels to confuse their pursuers. The treasure hunters shouted in frustration, splitting up to give chase. Emma ran alongside Max, their flashlights bouncing wildly as they navigated the labyrinthine passageways.

"They're right behind us!" Max panted.

"Keep going!" Emma urged. "We can't let them get the key!"

The chase was chaotic, the tunnels echoing with the sounds of footsteps and shouts. The siblings used every turn, every shadow, to their advantage, their knowledge of the map guiding them toward safety. Finally, after what felt like an eternity, they reached a small alcove and ducked inside, their breaths ragged and their hearts pounding.

"They're gone," Leo said, peeking out cautiously. "For now."

Emma turned to Max, who still clutched the Berlin Key tightly. "Are you okay?" she asked.

"Yeah," he said, though his hands were shaking. "But that was too close."

The siblings regrouped, their resolve stronger than ever. Dr. Klein's betrayal had shaken them, but it had also clarified their mission. The Core wasn't just a relic of the past—it was a battleground for the future.

And now, more than ever, they knew they couldn't let it fall into the wrong hands.

"Dr. Klein underestimated us," Emma said, her voice steady. "He thinks we're just kids. But we have something he doesn't."

"Each other," Ava said, her tone resolute.

Emma nodded. "And we're going to stop him—no matter what it takes."

As they pressed on toward Zone Theta, the Berlin Key secure in their possession, they knew the final showdown was near.

Chapter 26: The Flooded Tunnel

The air was colder in this part of the tunnels, carrying a dampness that clung to the siblings' skin. Their flashlights flickered against the moss-covered walls as the faint sound of trickling water grew louder with each step.

"I don't like this," Sophie said, her voice echoing slightly. "It feels... wrong."

"It's just water," Max said, though his own voice was uneasy. "We'll get through it."

Emma held up the map, the edges damp from the humid air. "The map shows this tunnel connects to the final passage leading to the Core," she said. "We don't have a choice—we have to go through."

Ava shone her flashlight ahead, illuminating the source of the sound: a pool of dark water stretching across the tunnel floor. The water rippled slightly, and the faint glimmer of debris floated near the edges.

"That's not just a puddle," Leo said, stepping forward to examine it. "It's deep."

"And getting deeper," Ava added, pointing to a steady trickle of water seeping in from cracks in the walls.

The siblings carefully approached the edge of the water. Emma crouched down, dipping her flashlight beam into the depths. The murky water reflected back only shadows, making it impossible to tell how far down it went.

"There's no other way," Emma said, her tone resolute. "We'll have to wade through."

"Wade?" Max asked, raising an eyebrow. "What if it's too deep?"

"We'll take it slow," Emma said. "Stay close, and keep an eye out for anything... unusual."

The siblings stepped into the water, the cold instantly biting at their legs. The floor beneath them was uneven, slick with algae and debris.

Each step was careful, their movements slow to avoid losing balance. The water quickly rose to their knees, then to their waists.

"Okay, this is officially awful," Sophie muttered, her flashlight clutched tightly in her hand.

"Keep moving," Emma urged, her eyes scanning the walls for any sign of danger—or a way out. "We're almost halfway."

As they moved deeper into the flooded tunnel, the trickle of water grew into a steady stream. The sound of rushing water filled the space, and the siblings realized with alarm that the water level was rising faster than they had expected.

"We need to hurry," Leo said, glancing back as the water reached his chest. "This isn't just a leak—it's flooding."

Emma nodded, her jaw tightening. "Stay together. If it gets too deep, we swim."

"Swim where?" Max asked, his voice rising. "We don't even know how far this goes!"

"Just trust me," Emma said, gripping his arm. "We're not stopping now."

The tunnel narrowed ahead, the walls closing in as the water surged higher. Sophie gasped as her flashlight slipped from her grasp, disappearing into the depths. "My light!" she cried.

"Stay calm!" Ava said, grabbing Sophie's hand. "We'll share mine."

The siblings pressed on, their breaths coming in shallow gasps as the water reached their necks. The tunnel seemed endless, the rising water making each step more treacherous. A sudden rush of cold sent a shiver through Emma as she felt the current tugging at her legs.

"There's a current," she said, her voice tense. "Stay close to the walls—use them for support."

As they inched forward, the sound of rushing water grew deafening. The siblings turned a corner and saw the source of the flood: a crack in the tunnel ceiling where water poured in like a waterfall, adding to the already rising levels.

"We're running out of time," Leo said, his face pale.

"There!" Ava shouted, pointing to a faint glimmer of light ahead. "It's an opening!"

Emma squinted, her heart lifting at the sight of a higher passageway just above the waterline. "That's our way out! Everyone, swim for it!"

The siblings swam against the current, their arms and legs straining as they pushed toward the opening. Debris floated around them, making each movement a battle. Emma reached the ledge first, gripping the slick stone and pulling herself up.

"Come on!" she shouted, reaching down to help Ava, who struggled against the current.

One by one, the siblings hauled themselves onto the ledge, gasping for air as the water continued to rise below them. Max was the last to climb up, his face flushed with exertion.

"Everyone okay?" Emma asked, her chest heaving.

"Define 'okay,'" Sophie muttered, wringing water from her sleeve.

The siblings sat in silence for a moment, their breath mingling with the humid air. The flooded tunnel below churned angrily, the sound of rushing water a constant reminder of how close they had come to disaster.

"We made it," Leo said finally, his voice shaky but relieved.

"But barely," Ava said, glancing at the map. "And we're not out of the woods yet."

Emma nodded, her resolve hardening. "This was just another test. Whatever's ahead, we're ready."

The siblings stood, their flashlights casting determined beams into the next passage. The Core was closer than ever, and they wouldn't let rising waters—or anything else—stop them now.

Chapter 27: The Guardian Mechanism

The passage beyond the flooded tunnel was quiet, the only sound the siblings' damp footsteps echoing softly off the walls. The air felt colder here, charged with an unexplainable energy that made the hair on the back of Emma's neck stand up.

As they rounded a corner, their flashlights illuminated a massive structure blocking the way forward. It was a towering, ancient-looking mechanism built into the tunnel walls, its surface engraved with intricate carvings and spirals that mirrored the designs on the Berlin Key. The metal gleamed faintly under their lights, as if untouched by time.

"What is that?" Sophie whispered, her voice tinged with awe.

"It looks like some kind of gate," Ava said, stepping closer. "Or... a machine."

"It's definitely more than just a door," Leo said, crouching to examine the base. "Look at these gears—they're massive. Whatever this is, it's designed to move. Or activate."

Emma's eyes scanned the carvings. "It's a guardian," she said, her voice certain. "A last line of defence to protect whatever is beyond it."

At the center of the mechanism was a circular slot, its design unmistakable.

"It's the Berlin Key," Max said, pulling the key from his bag. "This slot matches it perfectly."

"Wait," Emma said, holding up her hand. "We don't know what activating this will do."

Leo pointed to an inscription etched above the slot, the text written in a mix of German and what appeared to be an older, symbolic script. "There's a message here," he said, pulling out his notebook. "Give me a second to translate."

As Leo worked, the others studied the mechanism. The carvings depicted scenes of people fleeing, others working at machines, and a glowing sphere that bore a striking resemblance to the Core.

"It's a warning," Ava said, tracing one of the carvings. "Look at this—these people aren't just running; they're terrified."

"It's like they were trying to protect themselves from something," Sophie added, her flashlight lingering on a carving of a crumbling structure.

Leo stood up, his face pale as he finished translating. "It says, 'Only the worthy may proceed. The unworthy shall face the wrath of the guardian.'"

"Wrath?" Max repeated. "That's... not comforting."

Emma's brow furrowed. "It's a test. This mechanism isn't just a gate—it's a challenge. If we activate it and fail, there's a good chance something dangerous will happen."

"Like what?" Sophie asked.

Leo gestured to the carvings. "Given the scale of this thing? Probably traps. Or worse."

Emma studied the key in Max's hand, then turned to the others. "We don't have a choice," she said. "If this is the only way forward, we have to try."

"But what if we're not 'worthy'?" Ava asked. "What does that even mean?"

Emma took a deep breath. "I think it means working together. Every step of this journey has tested us—as a team, as a family. If we approach this the way we've handled everything else, we can get through it."

The siblings exchanged determined glances, their fear giving way to resolve.

"Let's do it," Max said, stepping forward with the key.

Max inserted the Berlin Key into the slot and turned it slowly. The mechanism groaned to life, its gears grinding and shifting as the carvings began to glow with a faint blue light. The floor beneath their feet vibrated, and a deep hum resonated through the chamber.

"Something's happening," Sophie said, her eyes wide.

The central part of the mechanism began to rotate, revealing a series of levers, buttons, and symbols etched into a circular panel. Above the panel, three glowing orbs appeared, their light casting eerie shadows across the room.

"It's a puzzle," Leo said, examining the panel. "The symbols match the ones from the map. We have to align them correctly to pass."

"And if we don't?" Max asked.

Leo glanced nervously at the glowing orbs. "Then we probably trigger whatever 'wrath' the inscription was talking about."

The siblings worked quickly, combining their knowledge to decipher the puzzle. Ava identified the symbols, matching them to their corresponding sections of the map. Leo manipulated the levers, aligning the gears with the glowing orbs, while Emma directed the sequence based on their findings.

The hum of the mechanism grew louder with each move, the room trembling as if testing their resolve. The carvings on the walls seemed to shift and move, their glowing patterns pulsing in time with the orbs.

"We're almost there," Leo said, sweat beading on his forehead. "One more sequence."

Emma studied the remaining symbols, her heart racing. "Ava, is this one the spiral or the double lines?"

"Spiral," Ava said without hesitation. "It's tied to the Berlin Key's design."

Leo adjusted the final lever, the symbols aligning perfectly. For a moment, the room fell silent, the hum fading into an eerie stillness.

Then, with a resounding clunk, the mechanism unlocked. The central panel slid open, revealing a narrow passage glowing with the same blue light as the Core.

"We did it," Sophie said, her voice filled with relief.

The siblings stepped back, the Berlin Key still secure in the mechanism. As the glowing orbs dimmed, the carvings on the walls seemed to relax, their light fading into darkness.

"We're through," Emma said, leading the way into the passage. "But that was just the guardian. Whatever's ahead—it's the real test."

With the guardian mechanism behind them, the siblings pressed forward, the blue light guiding them toward the heart of Zone Theta—and the Core that lay at its center.

Chapter 28: The Betrayal

The glow of the Core filled the chamber with an eerie, pulsating light, casting shifting shadows on the walls. The siblings stood in awe, their breaths caught as they took in the massive energy sphere suspended in midair, cables snaking outward like veins feeding into the surrounding machinery. The faint hum of its power resonated in their chests, a reminder of the immense energy contained within.

"This is it," Emma said, her voice barely above a whisper. "The Elysium Core."

"We made it," Max added, his gaze fixed on the swirling patterns of light within the sphere. "Now what?"

Before Emma could respond, a sudden noise behind them made them all spin around. The sound of footsteps echoed through the tunnel leading into the chamber, followed by a familiar voice.

"Well done, kids."

Dr. Klein stepped into the light, flanked by Carter and several members of the rival group. The treasure hunters looked rough, their faces smeared with dirt and their weapons visible at their sides, but their eyes gleamed with triumph as they took in the sight of the Core.

"You led us straight to it," Carter said, his tone mocking. "Good job."

Emma's fists clenched as she stepped in front of her siblings. "We're not letting you take it," she said firmly.

Dr. Klein smirked, his eyes flicking toward the Core. "Take it? My dear, you misunderstand. We're not just taking it—we're harnessing it. This energy source is the key to reshaping the future, and it belongs to those who know how to use it."

"Like you?" Sophie shot back. "You don't even understand what it is. All you care about is power."

Dr. Klein's smile faded. "Power is exactly what the world needs. The Core's energy can provide infinite possibilities—clean energy, advanced technology. And if it requires a little risk to unlock that potential, so be it."

Carter raised a hand, his men stepping forward. "Enough talk," he said. "Hand over the key."

Emma shook her head, her voice steady. "No. The Core is unstable. If you try to activate it, you'll put everyone at risk."

Dr. Klein scoffed. "Risk is part of progress."

As the treasure hunters advanced, Max and Leo stepped in front of Emma, their stances protective. "You'll have to go through us," Max said.

"That can be arranged," Carter replied, pulling a weapon from his holster.

Before he could act, a sudden vibration rippled through the chamber. The Core's hum grew louder, the swirling patterns within it accelerating. The light shifted, glowing brighter and casting harsh shadows across the room.

"What's happening?" Ava asked, her voice tinged with panic.

Emma glanced at the Core, her stomach sinking. "They're destabilizing it. Just by being here, they're interfering with the containment field."

Dr. Klein's expression shifted to one of alarm as the Core's light flared, bathing the room in a harsh white glow. "What did you do?" he demanded, turning to Emma.

"It's not us—it's you!" she shouted. "The Core isn't meant to be approached like this. If you don't stop, it'll overload!"

Carter ignored her warning, stepping closer to the Core. "If it's that powerful, then it's worth the risk. Let's see what this thing can really do."

"Don't touch it!" Leo shouted, but it was too late.

One of Carter's men reached for the console near the Core, pressing a button in a bid to activate the sphere. The effect was immediate: the Core's hum turned into a deafening roar, and a shockwave rippled outward, knocking everyone to the ground.

Sparks flew from the surrounding machinery as the Core's light intensified, its swirling patterns becoming chaotic and unstable. The room shook violently, debris falling from the ceiling as the energy surged.

"This is bad!" Max shouted, helping Ava to her feet. "Really bad!"

Dr. Klein scrambled to his feet, his calm demeanour shattered. "You fools! You've triggered the failsafe!"

"What failsafe?" Carter demanded, his voice rising in panic.

Emma's mind raced as she grabbed the Berlin Key from her bag. "The failsafe is designed to prevent the Core from being misused. If it detects interference, it destabilizes itself—and takes everything with it."

Chaos erupted as the treasure hunters realized the danger. Carter and his men abandoned their bravado, scrambling for the exit as the chamber continued to quake. Dr. Klein hesitated, his gaze flicking between the Core and the siblings.

"This isn't over," he said, his voice low. "The Core is too valuable to destroy."

"You're not getting another chance," Emma shot back. "Not after this."

Dr. Klein disappeared into the tunnels, leaving the siblings alone with the raging Core.

"We have to shut it down," Leo said, his voice urgent.

"How?" Sophie asked, shielding her face from the blinding light. "It's out of control!"

Emma held up the Berlin Key, her fingers trembling. "There's a control panel near the base. If we use the key, we might be able to re-engage the containment field."

"It's worth a shot," Max said, steadying her. "Let's do it."

The siblings moved together, fighting against the surging energy as they approached the control panel. Emma inserted the Berlin Key into the slot, the mechanism groaning as it activated.

The control panel lit up, displaying a series of symbols and levers. Leo worked quickly, his fingers flying over the controls as he deciphered the sequence. "We need to align the containment field with the Core's energy output," he said. "If we don't get it right, it'll explode."

"Just tell us what to do," Ava said, her voice steady despite the chaos.

Leo guided them through the process, each sibling taking a lever or button to stabilize the Core. The sphere's light flickered, the chaotic patterns slowing as the containment field began to re-engage.

"We're almost there!" Emma shouted. "Keep going!"

With a final adjustment, the Core's light dimmed, and the hum subsided into a low, steady pulse. The room stilled, the vibrations fading as the containment field fully re-engaged.

The siblings collapsed to the ground, their breaths ragged. For a moment, there was only silence, broken by the faint hum of the stabilized Core.

"We did it," Sophie said, her voice trembling. "We stopped it."

"But for how long?" Ava asked, glancing at the glowing sphere.

Emma stood, her resolve hardening. "Long enough to make sure no one else can get to it."

Chapter 29: The Energy Source Revealed

The chamber had fallen eerily silent after the Core stabilized, the hum of its energy now a faint, rhythmic pulse. The siblings sat in a circle near the base of the Core, their flashlights casting long shadows across the room. The initial shock of their near-disaster was beginning to fade, replaced by a profound curiosity about the enigmatic sphere before them.

"We almost died protecting it," Max said, breaking the silence. "But do we even know what 'it' is?"

"It's not just energy," Leo said, gesturing toward the Core. "This thing is way more advanced than anything we've ever seen. It's not just a machine—it's a breakthrough."

Emma stood, brushing dust from her hands as she approached the console near the Core. "The documents in the archive said the Core was meant to power underground facilities," she said. "But they also hinted at something bigger."

"Like what?" Ava asked, her voice steady despite the lingering tension.

"Let's find out," Emma said. She inserted the Berlin Key into the console, her fingers brushing the controls. The interface lit up, its ancient screen displaying text in German and symbols that mirrored the patterns on the Core.

Leo stepped up beside her, scanning the display. "It's a diagnostic readout," he said, translating quickly. "This section shows energy output levels... and this one—"

He paused, his eyes widening. "This isn't just a power source. It's a prototype for a clean energy system."

"What kind of clean energy?" Max asked, leaning in.

Leo's voice was tinged with awe as he read the text aloud. "The Core generates self-sustaining energy using advanced principles of fusion and quantum mechanics. It's designed to produce limitless power with zero waste or emissions."

"Limitless power?" Sophie repeated, her tone incredulous. "That's impossible."

"It's not," Leo said, pointing to the glowing sphere. "This proves it. They built it, and it works."

Ava stepped closer, her gaze fixed on the Core. "If this is true... this isn't just a treasure. It's a solution. To energy crises, to climate change, to so many problems we're facing right now."

"That's why they buried it," Emma said, her voice steady. "It's too powerful. In the wrong hands, it could be exploited—or turned into a weapon."

"But in the right hands," Leo countered, "it could change everything."

The siblings fell silent, the weight of the discovery settling over them. The Core wasn't gold, jewels, or a forgotten relic. It was something far more valuable: the potential to reshape the future.

Sophie crossed her arms, her expression conflicted. "So what do we do? We can't just leave it here—it's too important."

"But we can't take it with us," Ava said. "Even if we could move it, the technology is decades ahead of its time. No one would know how to use it safely."

Emma nodded, her mind racing. "We need to make sure it stays hidden. At least until the world is ready for it."

"And how do we do that?" Max asked. "The treasure hunters won't stop looking. Neither will Klein."

Emma stepped back to the console, scrolling through the interface. "The containment protocols. There's a way to seal the Core permanently. We can lock it behind layers of defences—more than what we've already seen. If anyone tries to get close, the Core will deactivate itself."

As the siblings worked together to initiate the protocols, the console displayed a final confirmation: "Permanent Containment Sequence—Confirm Activation?"

Emma looked at her siblings, her hand hovering over the button. "This is it. Once we do this, the Core stays locked away—maybe forever."

Leo nodded. "It's the right choice. If someone finds it before they're ready, the consequences could be catastrophic."

"Do it," Max said, his voice firm.

Emma pressed the button. The chamber began to hum, the sound growing into a low, resonant vibration. The Core's light dimmed slightly as the containment field intensified, its energy pulsing in slow, steady waves. The walls around them shifted, hidden panels sliding into place to encase the Core in layers of protective shielding.

When the sequence was complete, the chamber fell silent again, the Core's faint glow visible through the translucent shielding. The siblings stepped back, their breaths steady as they took in the sight of the now-contained energy source.

"It's done," Emma said, her voice soft but resolute.

"For now," Sophie said. "But what about the future? What if someone tries to find it again?"

Emma looked at the Berlin Key in her hand, its intricate design glinting in the light. "We make sure they can't. The Key stays with us, and the map goes somewhere no one will ever find it."

As they prepared to leave the chamber, the siblings paused for one last look at the Core. It wasn't the treasure they had expected, but it was far more important. It was a promise of what humanity could achieve—if they were ready.

Emma turned to her siblings, a faint smile breaking through her exhaustion. "We did something good here," she said. "Something that matters."

"And we did it together," Ava added, her voice filled with quiet pride.

Chapter 30: The Collapse

The tremor hit with no warning, sending a cascade of dust and debris raining down from the ceiling. The ground shifted violently beneath their feet, throwing the siblings and the treasure hunters to the ground. A deafening crack echoed through the tunnels as part of the ceiling gave way, sealing the passage behind them with a wall of stone.

"Everyone okay?" Emma shouted, her voice barely audible over the rumbling.

"I'm fine," Ava called, coughing through the dust.

"Still breathing!" Max replied, pulling Sophie to her feet.

Dr. Klein stepped forward, his face pale but determined. "We don't have time to check. The entire tunnel system is unstable. If we don't move now, none of us are getting out."

The group stumbled forward, their flashlights barely cutting through the thick haze of dust. The air grew heavy and stale, each breath feeling like an effort. As they rounded a corner, a second tremor rippled through the tunnels, dislodging another section of the ceiling.

"Look out!" Carter shouted, pushing one of his men out of the way as a massive stone crashed to the ground.

"We're running out of time," Leo said, his voice tight with fear. "This whole place is coming down."

Emma glanced at the map, her hands trembling. "There's a side tunnel ahead. It's a tight squeeze, but it leads to the main exit."

"Then let's go!" Max said, already moving toward the passage.

The side tunnel was narrow, the walls pressing in on either side as they crawled through. Dr. Klein was the last to enter, his sharp eyes scanning the unstable structure behind them. He hesitated for a moment, then followed, the ceiling groaning ominously above.

As they emerged into a slightly wider passage, Leo pointed toward a faint glow in the distance. "That's the way out," he said, relief colouring his voice.

But before they could move, another tremor struck. The tunnel quaked violently, and a section of the passage ahead began to collapse, sending a wall of rubble crashing down to block their path.

"We're trapped," Sophie said, panic rising in her voice. "What do we do now?"

Dr. Klein stepped forward, his gaze fixed on the unstable ceiling. "There's a manual release for the emergency gate up there," he said, pointing to a rusted mechanism embedded in the wall. "If we activate it, it will stabilize this section long enough for you to get through."

"But that's good, right?" Ava asked. "We can activate it and all get out."

Dr. Klein shook his head, his expression grim. "The release requires constant pressure to hold. Once it's activated, someone has to stay behind to keep it engaged."

"No," Emma said immediately, stepping in front of him. "We'll find another way."

"There is no other way," Dr. Klein said, his voice firm. "If we don't do this, everyone dies."

Carter approached, his face hard. "You're not doing this alone," he said. "We'll help hold it open."

"You'll barely hold it for five minutes," Dr. Klein replied. "You'd never make it out alive. I know how this system works—I can buy you enough time to escape."

Emma grabbed his arm, her eyes blazing. "There has to be another way. You don't have to do this."

Dr. Klein's expression softened, a flicker of regret passing through his eyes. "I've spent my life chasing power, thinking I could control it. But today, I've learned there's more to protect than ambition. Let me do this. It's my choice."

With a heavy heart, Emma stepped back, her hands trembling. "Thank you," she said, her voice breaking. "For saving us."

Dr. Klein nodded, a faint smile on his lips. "Make sure the Core stays hidden. Don't let anyone else repeat my mistakes."

He turned to the manual release, gripping the lever with both hands. As he pulled it down, a deafening clang echoed through the chamber. The ceiling above the exit stabilized, and the rubble shifted slightly, creating a narrow gap large enough to crawl through.

"Go!" Dr. Klein shouted over the rumbling. "I can hold it!"

The siblings moved quickly, scrambling through the narrow opening. Carter and his men followed, their usual bravado replaced by solemn determination. One by one, they emerged into the fresh air outside, collapsing onto the ground as the final tremor shook the tunnels behind them.

Emma turned back toward the entrance, her heart aching as the ground settled. The tunnel was silent now, the faint glow of the emergency gate the only sign of Dr. Klein's sacrifice.

"He did it," Ava said softly, tears streaming down her face. "He saved us."

"He redeemed himself," Leo added, his voice heavy with emotion. "In the end, he chose to do the right thing."

Emma stood, her gaze fixed on the collapsed tunnel. "We'll honour him," she said. "And we'll make sure no one ever finds the Core."

As the siblings walked away from the site, the weight of their journey settled over them. They had uncovered a secret that could change the world and witnessed the ultimate sacrifice of a man seeking redemption. Together, they vowed to protect the Core's secret, carrying the lessons of their journey with them.

The tunnels behind them were silent now, but the memory of what had happened—and what they had gained—would stay with them forever.

Chapter 31: The Warning

The morning sun broke through the horizon as the siblings stood at the edge of the collapsed tunnel, the weight of their journey pressing heavily on their shoulders. The cool breeze carried the faint smell of earth and stone, a reminder of the dangers they had just escaped.

Emma knelt near a weathered signpost at the tunnel's entrance, her fingers tracing the old, rusted lettering. The site had been abandoned for decades, its secrets buried deep within the underground labyrinth. But she knew it wasn't enough to rely on time and obscurity to keep the treasure hunters away.

"They'll come back," Emma said quietly, her gaze fixed on the rubble. "People like Carter, they'll keep searching. And they might get further than we did."

"We can't let that happen," Ava said, her voice resolute.

"We won't," Emma replied, pulling out a notebook and pencil. "We're leaving a warning. Something only those who understand the danger will recognize."

The siblings huddled together, brainstorming a message that would be clear to those with the knowledge to decode it, but cryptic enough to deter the unprepared. Ava sketched symbols from the Berlin Key and the Core's containment seals, combining them into a design that spoke of secrecy and caution.

Leo added a set of coordinates to the design, ones that led to empty ground far from the actual site of the Core. "It's a misdirection," he explained. "If anyone tries to follow this, they'll end up nowhere."

Sophie wrote the text of the warning, her words chosen carefully:

"Beneath these stones lies more than history. For those who seek, know this: the prize is destruction, not salvation. Turn back, for some treasures are meant to remain hidden."

Emma studied the message, her jaw tightening. "It's good," she said. "But we need more than words."

"We'll use the symbols," Ava said, pointing to her sketch. "The spirals, the runes—everything that ties back to the Core's warnings. They'll act as a seal, something even treasure hunters might hesitate to disturb."

Leo nodded, his expression thoughtful. "And we should add a fail-safe. If someone does manage to figure out the message and tries to dig deeper, they'll hit a dead end—or something that slows them down."

Max looked up from his work clearing debris around the entrance. "A physical warning. Something unmistakable."

The siblings worked for hours, carving the warning into a large, flat stone they found near the tunnel's entrance. The symbols Ava had drawn were etched deeply into its surface, the text of Sophie's message placed beneath them in stark, bold letters. They mounted the stone at the edge of the collapse, ensuring it would be the first thing anyone saw if they stumbled upon the site.

"It's done," Emma said, stepping back to admire their work. "This will deter anyone who comes looking."

"And if it doesn't?" Sophie asked.

"Then they'll face the same challenges we did," Max said. "And hopefully, they'll turn back before it's too late."

As the siblings prepared to leave, Emma placed the Berlin Key back into her bag. Its intricate spirals gleamed faintly in the morning light, a reminder of the power they had protected and the responsibility they now carried.

"We're the guardians now," Emma said, her voice steady. "It's up to us to make sure no one unlocks that door again."

The others nodded, their bond stronger than ever after the trials they had faced. Together, they turned away from the site, leaving the coded warning behind as their final act of protection.

The underground network would remain undisturbed, its secrets buried for generations to come. And as the siblings walked toward the horizon, they knew their adventure wasn't just about what they had discovered—it was about what they had safeguarded for the future.

Chapter 32: Home Again

The Edmondson house was quiet that evening, the warm glow of the setting sun streaming through the windows. Outside, the leaves of the old oak tree in the yard rustled softly in the breeze, the calm a stark contrast to the chaos of the past few days.

Emma sat cross-legged on the couch, the Berlin Key resting in her palm. She turned it over slowly, the intricate spirals catching the light. Each groove and symbol carried the weight of their journey, a reminder of the secrets they had uncovered—and the responsibility they now bore.

"You're still staring at that thing?" Max teased, leaning against the doorway with a sandwich in hand. "You're going to burn a hole in it with your eyes."

Emma managed a small smile. "It's hard not to. This little key could've changed everything. And maybe it still will—just not in the way anyone expected."

Ava entered the room, carrying her sketchbook. She flopped onto the armchair, flipping through the pages filled with hurried drawings and notes from their adventure. "It feels weird being home after all that," she said. "Like... did it even happen?"

"It happened," Leo said, walking in with his laptop. He pulled up a file containing the digital copies of the maps, schematics, and warnings they had created to preserve the Core's secrets. "We've got the proof. And a whole lot of lessons to go with it."

Sophie joined them, curling up on the couch beside Emma. "Do you think anyone will ever find it again?" she asked, her voice soft. "The Core, I mean."

Emma placed the Berlin Key on the coffee table, her gaze thoughtful. "Maybe. But not without the right intentions. That warning we left, the failsafe's we activated—they'll make sure of it."

Max plopped down onto the floor, leaning back against the couch. "It's crazy to think about," he said. "We stood in front of something that could power the world—or destroy it. And we chose to keep it hidden."

"Because the world isn't ready," Ava said firmly. "And we weren't about to let people like Carter decide when it would be."

Leo nodded. "Still, it makes you wonder. What if, one day, someone finds it and uses it for good? What if the Core does change the world?"

"It already changed ours," Sophie said, her voice filled with quiet conviction.

The room fell into a comfortable silence as the siblings reflected on her words. Their adventure had tested them in ways they never imagined, pushing them to the limits of their courage, ingenuity, and trust in one another. They had faced danger, betrayal, and the unknown—and they had emerged stronger, bound by their shared experience.

"We're different now," Emma said finally, her voice steady. "And maybe that's the point. The Core wasn't just a discovery—it was a lesson. About power, about responsibility, and about what really matters."

Max smirked. "And what really matters is that we're awesome."

The room erupted in laughter, the tension of their recent ordeal melting away.

Later that evening, as the house grew quiet again, Emma stood at the window, gazing out at the stars. Her siblings had gone to bed, their exhaustion finally catching up with them. But Emma's mind was still racing, filled with thoughts of the journey they had just completed—and the mysteries that still lay ahead.

The Berlin Key glinted faintly on the coffee table, its presence a reminder of their role as guardians. Emma knew their adventure wasn't the end of the story. Somewhere, other secrets waited to be uncovered, other challenges to be faced.

As she turned off the lights and headed upstairs, a faint smile crossed her face. Whatever came next, they would face it together. The Edmondsons weren't just siblings—they were a team. And the world was full of mysteries waiting for them to solve.

For now, though, they were home. And that was enough.

Disclaimer

This book is a work of fiction. While inspired by real locations, historical events, and underground sites in Berlin, the story, characters, and specific details of the underground network, artifacts, and events are entirely products of the author's imagination.

Any resemblance to actual persons, living or dead, organizations, or events is purely coincidental. The portrayal of Berlin's underground is fictionalized for the purposes of the narrative and should not be considered an accurate depiction of the city's historical or modern structures.

Readers are encouraged to explore Berlin's rich history and underground sites responsibly and with proper guidance, as real locations may contain hazards or restricted areas. All historical interpretations in this book are fictionalized for entertainment and storytelling purposes.